CREOLA'S MOONBEAM

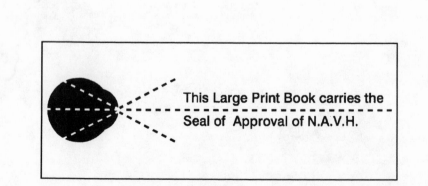

This Large Print Book carries the
Seal of Approval of N.A.V.H.

CREOLA'S MOONBEAM

MILAM McGRAW PROPST

THORNDIKE PRESS

An imprint of Thomson Gale, a part of The Thomson Corporation

Detroit • New York • San Francisco • New Haven, Conn. • Waterville, Maine • London

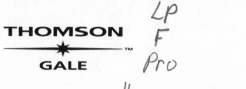

THOMSON
GALE
™

*LP
F
Pro*

#395151100453382

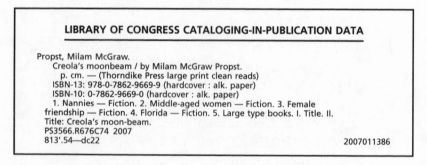

LIBRARY OF CONGRESS CATALOGING-IN-PUBLICATION DATA

Propst, Milam McGraw.
  Creola's moonbeam / by Milam McGraw Propst.
    p. cm. — (Thorndike Press large print clean reads)
  ISBN-13: 978-0-7862-9669-9 (hardcover : alk. paper)
  ISBN-10: 0-7862-9669-0 (hardcover : alk. paper)
  1. Nannies — Fiction. 2. Middle-aged women — Fiction. 3. Female
friendship — Fiction. 4. Florida — Fiction. 5. Large type books. I. Title. II.
Title: Creola's moon-beam.
PS3566.R676C74 2007
813'.54—dc22   2007011386

Published in 2007 by arrangement with BelleBooks, Inc.

Printed in the United States of America on permanent paper
10 9 8 7 6 5 4 3 2 1

Dedication

On the occasion of her 90th birthday, July 23, 2004, I am indeed honored to dedicate my new book, *Creola's Moonbeam,* to my cousin and dear friend, Ociee Annette Nash Robnett.

Poet, family historian, musician, mother, wife, and grandmother, Ociee Annette has been a gift to me. A model of courage, endurance, and strength, she follows in the footsteps of her aunt and namesake, my grandmother, Ociee Nash Whitman.

CHAPTER 1

Creola Moon was butterscotch in color and built like a biscuit, the flakey kind of biscuit that has lots and lots of layers. She and her family had come to Georgia from the exotic realm of New Orleans. Creola's distinctive grin — missing a tooth — filled most of her pie-round face. Her zebra-striped hair made her easy to spot each morning as she walked the short block down the tree-shaded Georgia street and into my anxious arms. I was a small white girl, and she was the large black nanny who raised me.

Creola was the first and most dear friend I made. She remained in my life for nearly fifty years as a confidante, mentor, encourager, and advisor. It was Creola who taught me the art of storytelling. I called her *Crellie.*

Crellie rarely called me and my sister by our given names, Harriette and Mary Pearle. She coined *Moonbeam* as her special name for me, while my sister became *Price-less Pearlie.* We girls loved the fun and the mystery of having unique names. I, most especially.

To me, she was my Crellie. I was her Moonbeam.

I admit it: I talk to her spirit. A grown woman, talking to ghosts. For one thing, I'm old enough that I don't always sleep soundly. Years of listening for babies to cry and for teenage drivers to pull up in the driveway laid that groundwork.

Today, for example, I woke up in my suburban Atlanta home well before the sun. My husband, Beau, was away on a business trip. *Woke up.* That's a lie. I'd been awake most of the night tossing and turning, thinking, making trips to the bathroom, drinking water, and returning to bed to repeat the pattern. My decision was firm.

Sliding out of bed, I jumped into my warm-up suit and running shoes. I grabbed my latest manuscript from the bedside table, tiptoed down the hall, and hurried out the kitchen door. Lifting the garbage can lid, I hurled the papers into a smelly stew of last night's meat loaf, coffee grounds, egg shells, rice, and butter beans.

"Good riddance to you!"

Flashlight in hand, I headed out for a

long, quiet dawn walk. I needed the exercise. I also wanted to remove myself from the temptation of going back to rescue eight weeks of fruitless writing. The truth be told, my book of short stories read like garbage. The hodgepodge, whose sole connection was the same typeface, Arial, belonged in a galvanized can.

Two hours later, I stood sipping hot green tea and watched as the sanitation worker dumped the trash into the back of his truck. The always warm and cheerful man secured his load under the tarp and grinned at me. His white teeth gleamed in the early morning sunshine.

" 'Mornin', Miz Newberry."

What my heart heard him say was, *Sure you want me to take this to the dump? After all, you did work eight long weeks on it.*

Stop! I *almost* shouted.

What came out was, "Good morning to you."

Beep, beep, beep, beep. His truck rolled backwards down our drive. Several pages of my manuscript flew out from underneath the tarp, gravy-stained and peppered with flecks of coffee grounds. I noticed the print was faded to a blur.

A blur. The perfect analogy.

A squirrel scampered across my feet.

Surprised, I jumped back. Then I addressed the bushy-tailed rodent, admitting the truth to him-or-her, and to myself.

"I never could knit together those *dern* stories." Balling up the escaped pages, I tossed them back into the empty trash can. Slam dunk. *Hooray.*

I went back inside, walked to my desk, turned on the computer, and pulled up a file. Mouthing a drum roll — *Da, da DA* — I pressed *delete.*

Honey Butlar Newberry's book of short stories. Gone.

I wondered, do other writers respond to failure with such drama? If I could author an entire book, why couldn't I perform the simple feat of weaving together a few stories about my family and our house? In the beginning, the idea sounded easy enough.

Then I freaked out.

Regret gripped me. I considered the numerous events I'd missed because of my self-imposed commitment to get those stories published. Alas. Neglected visits with friends and family, lost time with my husband, ignored art shows, and far too many unseen movies. Egads, I'd even bailed out of our bridge club's annual girls' trip. A major mistake.

My remorse intensified as I tallied up the

calories ingested from boxes of crackers, nuts, and cookies, not to mention the harmful caffeine in the gallons of tea and diet cola drunk. My net weight gain was eight pounds or one pound per week. Groaning, I clutched my well-defined love handles. Pinch an inch? What rhymes with "fistful?"

And fun? None.

All for what? My project was en route to garbage hell while its computer file floated aimlessly in cyberspace.

After a few moments of irrational planning, I vetoed going out to the Fulton County garbage dump. Honey Newberry, a fifty-some-odd-year-old writer with three-inch roots of gray hair, climbing over mounds of other folks' refuse, did not paint a pretty picture. Having my hair colored was something else I'd failed to schedule during my writing binge.

I then chastised myself for not recycling. If I'd only separated the paper from the cans, like a good citizen, then I could have so easily driven out to the county's recycling center to retrieve the manuscript. No smelly garbage to crawl through, just paper, mounds and mounds of it, but paper, nonetheless.

Sadly, recycling was no longer an option for the Newberry family. My fault, too.

A few weeks prior, as I'd hurriedly backed out of the driveway in my Jeep, I rolled over the regulation green plastic bin, completely destroying it. I replaced the bin with a blue one from the hardware store, but it seems that was unacceptable. *They* only pick up what's in *their* containers, which ended the Newberry family's single environmentally correct habit. Ever since, all the trash, plastics, old newspapers, spoiled food, and dead chipmunks had been relegated to the same dismal destination — the galvanized can outside the back door.

I digress.

At present, the computer felt like a heavy ball and chain to me. Thoughts of putting my fingers back on the keyboard made me cringe. I was far more enthusiastic about other activities. There were friends to meet for lunch, the kitchen to paint, my family to enjoy, a new sofa to purchase, and my most favorite work-related activity of all, giving talks. My calendar had several scheduled. I checked. *Ah hah.* I had one on Thursday week.

Feeling out of control — likely due to a total lack of sleep — I attempted a more productive dialogue with myself. A therapist might call it an *affirmation.* To me, it was simply Creola talk.

*Look at you, Miss Moonbeam! You're run-
ning around this house acting as foolish as a
goose. You best quit second-guessing yourself. Now, get busy and show folks exactly
what you can do! Get back to your writing!*

"Not this time, ma'am," I said aloud. "I
have a speech to give."

Typically, my audiences are made up of
adults, generally adult women, many of
whom have already read my books. Some
are even eager to meet the author. I feel like
something of a rock star on those occasions.

This was different, however; these were
children. Children are unpredictable. They
unnerve me. When I give speeches to children, I am a wreck.

Not only is my audience children, they
were middle-school students. For me, it's
much easier to talk with two hundred adults
than it is to communicate with five young
people. There I stood at the podium with
three-hundred-fifty pairs of eyes — teacher-
coerced eyes — politely awaiting my appearance.

Shaking in my shoes, I certainly intended
to do my best. Children are scary, yes, but
they are also ever so important to me. There
could be a promising writer, another Mar-

garet Mitchell, in the group. I had a responsibility.

Right, Creola?

Carry on, Moonbeam, I could hear her saying. Her encouragement sustained me.

My friend Martha, the teacher who'd invited me, began her introduction. "Mrs. Newberry is our Career Day speaker, a special lady, and a *real* author." As Martha continued, I smiled confidently and secretly wondered about whom she was saying such nice things. I laughed to myself. If only those trusting teachers and their bright-eyed middle-schoolers had witnessed my recent creative meltdown, they'd have bolted from the school auditorium.

Martha was about to conclude her part of the program. How *was* I to act? Surely as a professional. Down to earth, approachable? Or should I behave like a famous person, one who is completely "cool and with it?" To begin with, I didn't feel famous. Secondly, using those words, "cool and with it" told me I definitely was *not.* I ultimately went with being myself.

As any practiced speaker feigning confidence will do, I took the microphone, looked pleasantly into the sea of faces, and began. I talked about creative writing, about the value of keeping journals, about being

14

persistent in the face of rejection, about character development, and so on. Things went fine. I concluded my talk and asked if there were any questions. Pleasantly surprised at the teenagers' enthusiasm, I happily responded to their queries concerning the characters in two of my books.

Had I a favorite character?

That was easy. "My grandmother, the heroine in my first novel." I urged the audience, students, and teachers alike, to write their own stories about older persons they loved.

A hand flew high, and a young lady breathlessly announced, "I already have, Mrs. Newberry. I wrote a story about my dad, who is *reeeallly* old. When he was a little boy, he only had three channels on his TV!"

The young people ohhhed and ahhhhed.

I countered, "Guess what? My family didn't even *own* a television until I was six-years-old!"

Silence.

I may as well have told the audience I'd arrived by ship. Was it the *Nina,* the *Pinta,* or the *Santa Maria*?

Perhaps in a generous effort to help me salvage my reputation, one thoughtful eighth grader changed the subject by asking another question. "Mrs. Newberry, who inspired you when you were in school?"

Another obvious answer for me. "Why, my high school English teacher, Miss Kate. She was also our school newspaper's sponsor, and because of her, I worked for several papers before I began writing novels. Look around in this auditorium. I'm certain many of you have special teachers of your own. Thank you for the question; a good one!"

The students followed my advice. Some smiled at teachers, who glowed in response.

I was back on a roll.

A young man, a handsome fellow who bore a striking resemblance to Harry Potter, raised his hand. "Tell us please, Mrs. Newberry, what are you working on right now?"

I'd been caught. I wanted to interrogate him. *Young man, exactly who encouraged you to ask me* that *question? Was it a teacher? Was it my friend Martha?*

Wait a second; it was Creola, wasn't it! I'd always believed my beloved Crellie was more compassionate than that. Spirits are supposed to be compassionate, aren't they? Hold on, young man, do you know my sister? Ah ha, it was my older sister, Mary Pearle. She's been after me for months to finish my book of short stories. I just know

16

Mary Pearle ordered you to push me. The conniving shrew!

What I *did* say was even worse. I responded, "Another good question. Actually, I'm going to the beach next week and will return at summer's end with a book of short stories."

Who said that? Not me! Had I been possessed by Creola? I wanted to back away from the podium and sidle off the stage. Hundreds of eyes were on me, including the eyes of the teachers. *They can smell the truth, I thought.* I'd thrown the stories away. My tentative beach trip was planned exclusively for rest and relaxation. I was in trouble. Honey Newberry had told a big, fat lie! Now I was going to be *forced* to write more stories during the summer, because I'd made the announcement to an entire room full of trusting children!

Three weeks later, off to the beach I went. To rest. To work. To escape those probing eyes.

I could hear Creola chuckling.

CHAPTER 2

I stood in a condominium overlooking the beautiful Gulf beaches of Florida, but my attention was on myself. I'd left Beau at home in Atlanta, thankfully. Naked, I gazed into the bedroom mirror. Students, teachers, writing, family, war and famine, world chaos — those concerned me not. A crime had been committed. Someone had stolen my youthful body and replaced it with one of an aging fat woman.

The tag on my *Magik-Slim* promised my brand-new, magically slimming swimsuit would take off ten pounds. I was a desperate woman. I took the bathing suit from its shopping bag. Right foot, left foot. I stepped in, wriggling and tugging, until up over my thighs rolled the black, floral-splashed suit.

"Curses on all cookies and crackers. Curses on sitting too much, munching and typing. Curses on summer." Sucking in my stomach with a gasp, I jerked upward until

my ample form compressed into the *slim suit*. "It's magic all right. It's turned an ordinary woman into a giant bratwurst."

I wandered into the bathroom and viewed myself in that mirror. It was not a pretty sight. Each of the suit's orange, pink, and purple tropical blossoms had been strategically positioned to emphasize every major figure flaw — my ample butt, my small boobs, and my fat belly. Thank you, *Magik-Slim.*

I squeezed 50 SPF sunscreen onto my palm and slathered it over my lily-white body. Actually, that's lily-white with brown splotches, more akin to the hide of a giraffe. I remain determined to hold my own against a lifetime of well-earned sun damage. A childhood of unprotected play outside, coupled with the slathering on of iodine and baby oil, followed by college years devoted to tanning on the roof of the sorority house, had accomplished its mission.

That said, it frequently occurs to me that, were all the age spots to run together, I might just have the perfect tan. My unyielding dermatologist, Dr. Cox, vehemently disagrees with the concept.

Only when covered from forehead to toe with the cream, he insists, am I sufficiently protected from the rays of the sun. As usual,

Dr. Cox wins. Donning my floppy straw hat and long-sleeved white shirt, I paused to again view myself, this time in the entry hall mirror. Was I expecting an improvement?

I would lie to myself. Employ an affirmation.

"Fetching, Honey Newberry, you are positively fetching."

I sighed and headed outdoors. How I longed for the simplicity, and good skin, of my childhood at the beach.

But *that* was a story I'd thrown away.

1956, THE YEAR OF THE BATHING CAP

BY HONEY NEWBERRY

When I was a little girl, my older sister, Mary Pearle, and I could simply put on our bathing suits and run outside, slamming (always slamming) the rickety wooden door of the beach cottage's screened-in porch. Free as the wind, the two of us would charge through sugary white sand and splash into the cooling waters of the Gulf of Mexico.

There was no sunscreen for us and there was no need for hats. Nor, in the Fifties, was there any threat of a shark biting off our toes. Of course, sharks had always been around, but those frighteningly dangerous sea creatures never came near the pristine Gulf waters off St. George's Island where, for nearly two decades, we, the Butlar family, took our annual two-week vacation.

Wear hats? Not ever! That was true, with the exception of the summer of 1956, *The Year of the Bathing Cap.* A few weeks before our trip to the beach, Mary Pearle and I were thumbing through one of our mother's fashion magazines when we came across a lush tropical beach scene, one with swaying palm trees, pounding surf, beach umbrellas, and gorgeous models lounging about in sugar-white sand.

The models were wearing rubber bathing caps, but much to our surprise and admiration, these were not the frumpy black kind that older women like Mother wore. These stunning women sported fancy caps in a rainbow collection of color that coordinated with their swimsuits. Mary Pearle, at age thirteen, simply had to have one.

Wanting to do everything just like my older and more sophisticated sibling, I had to have one, too. I was eleven.

Mary Pearle went along with my wishes not because she respected my fashion sense, but because she was not about to be the only girl around wearing the trendy accessory. I was her ready disciple.

Giving in to our fervent and relentless pleadings, Mother agreed to take us shopping. As expected, however, such a chic item was hard to find in the modest stores of Humphrey, our small, middle-Georgia town. Much to our dismay, we came home empty-handed. Fortunately, however, only a couple of days before we were to leave on vacation, Mother hit pay dirt.

Mary Pearle and I were sitting on the living room rug putting together a one-hundred-piece puzzle, which, coincidentally, was a tropical scene. My sister and I — I especially — always daydreamed about the beach.

Mother burst in through the front door. She stopped and posed in a victory stance. Her high-heeled feet apart, in her gloved hands she triumphantly clutched a shopping bag.

"Eureka!" She emptied the bag and produced two identical swimming caps. Covered in pink petals and topped with green leaves, their design was even prettier than the ones in the magazine.

"Ohh, Mother, thank you, thank you!"

We jumped up, scattering the sand and surf puzzle pieces everywhere. My sister and I squealed with glee as we stuffed our long brown ponytails into the flowered caps. We hurried to admire ourselves in the hall-tree mirror.

Mary Pearle preened. "Look, Harriette, it will match my suit *puuurfectly.*"

"Mine, too."

Our mother beamed.

Our father, as he usually did, teased us,

"We'll surely be able to spot the two of you out in the water. Our darling daughters will be the only roses floating around with all those fish!"

"Oh, Daddy, you just don't understand," complained Mary Pearle. She was more anxious for his praise than for his good-natured teasing.

I had another concern. "I forgot about the fish, Daddy! I can't stand it when they swim into me. I wish we could have our Gulf without those slimy fish."

"Darling girl, it doesn't work that way. Besides, those fish are more afraid of you than you are of them."

"They couldn't be."

My sister wasn't worried about fish or me. She was too busy prancing about in her cap. It was five o'clock in the afternoon, nearly supper time, and good gracious sakes, if she didn't go and put on her swimsuit!

Daddy laughed at her. "Mary Pearle, are you expecting a flood?"

"Daaaddddeee! Mother, make him quit!"

Mother laughed, too.

Though still three years away from getting her driver's license, every time Mary Pearle Butlar wore her pink floral bathing cap she believed she was every bit as glamorous as

her favorite movie star, Elizabeth Taylor.
   I only prayed my cap wouldn't attract fish.

CHAPTER 3

My days of fearing fish are long gone. In truth, I believed Dr. Cox and his warnings about skin cancer. The sun was my enemy. The "well-seasoned" woman I'd become was far more focused on lotions to ward off that villain and on hats to make certain its rays didn't alter my newly quaffed and colored hair. Yes, I'd made it to the hairdresser before the trip to the beach. I no longer looked as if a calico cat sat perched atop my head.

During one Memorial Day family beach trip, Mary Pearle and I talked about aging. While Beau played golf, we sisters talked, we laughed, we ate, we shopped, and we delighted in our favorite activity — walking the beach. Despite some major disappointments in her life, my sister still maintained her deliciously dry sense of humor.

"Mary Pearle, have you noticed that your boobs are getting, hmmm, are they getting bigger?"

We were walking on the beach at the time. Mary Pearle stopped and turned to me. Putting her arm around my shoulders, she assumed a serious posture and cleared her throat. "No, little sister, they're not getting bigger. Just longer."

"Longer?"

"Longer."

For the rest of her visit, merely mouthing the word *longer* turned over my tickle box and Mary Pearle's as well.

All in all, I yearned for childhood, for its effortlessness, for the old cottage of those simple days, and mostly for my family, the family who had so contentedly vacationed inside.

I grimaced as I pushed the button for my condo's elevator. "Maybe it wouldn't be so bad if a shark were to take a small nip out of me. Depending on where he nibbled, of course." The fierce fish might trim a pound or two from my mid-section. A free liposuction of sorts.

The possibility of my losing twenty pounds of baby weight had long since passed. I have two children — a daughter, Mary Catherine, and her younger brother, Butlar. Butlar will turn twenty-four on his next birthday. I've carried those extra pregnancy pounds for a quarter of a century.

"Diet? Drat, I forgot my diet drink," I scurried back inside the condo. On the way out, I grabbed a handful of cheese crackers. "Energy for a brisk swim."

The smell of mildew hung like a damp cloud in the elevator. I attempted to hold my breath for the four-floor descent. "Can't," I gasped. I coughed in the dampness. Continuing my pattern of complaint, (perhaps due to my own sense of guilt for spending money to be there for the entire summer?) I thought about how cumbersome it was to carry all my necessities.

As a child, an old inner tube and favorite beach towel — the one with a pink poodle romping in the sand — were all the equipment required. Now I carried a towel, a folding chair, a drink, snacks, an umbrella, a new novel, lip-gloss, sunscreen, and my ever-present cell phone.

I reminded myself of an overburdened burro making the long trek into the Grand Canyon.

I caught my reflection in the elevator doors. Mirrors seem to be everywhere when one is feeling fat. "Am I shrinking to boot?" I wailed. "When did I become, well, so *compact?*" Alone in the smelly elevator I made yet another observation, "My bottom half is rising while my upper half is sinking."

The elevator stopped on the second floor.

"And good morning to you, too!" I responded to the cheery couple as they stepped on. "Yes, it's a perfectly marvelous day. I couldn't be better."

The elevator stopped on the first floor. "Go ahead," I motioned for them to exit ahead of me.

Taking another glimpse at myself, I muttered, "A pear on popsicle sticks, that's me."

I made my way toward the beach, following a wooden walkway across a sand dune. At the base of its wooden steps, I passed a shower and stepped onto the sand. The convenient beach shower is a modern marvel to me. No longer do vacationers have to deal with sand in their sheets and everywhere else! I admire that innovation every single time I pass an outdoor shower, because I can still hear my mother's constant vacation lament, "Harriette Ophelia Butlar! Mary Pearle Butlar! I just finished sweeping. Don't you two children be tracking any sand into this clean cottage!"

I was named for my mother's maiden aunts, Harriette and Ophelia. As a teenager, I believed with all my heart that, had the two dear old ladies been given more modern names, neither would have remained a spinster.

I must admit I was always envious of my sister's name, Mary Pearle. How often I wished that I'd been the firstborn and thus named for my glamorous aunt on our *father's* side, Mary Pearle Butlar Armstrong, who worked in the fashion industry in New York. Rarely had Daddy's baby sister returned to Georgia, but the couple of times she came, in the late 1950's, it was as if royalty had come to visit Humphrey.

I could hardly tolerate my sister during those few days. Being around her namesake aunt inflated her ego even more than usual.

"Mary Pearle Butlar, you are acting like *you* are the fancy lady from New York City," I'd complain. "You are nothing but a plain little Georgia girl, a little girl from Humphrey, exactly like me!"

Didn't do a bit of good. She'd stick out her tongue and priss away with her nose stuck straight up in the air.

I loved Aunt Harriette and Aunt Ophelia. Those fine Southern ladies could not have been any dearer to me, but never once did I plan to turn out like either of *my* namesakes.

When I grew up — having spent the first twenty-two years of my life as *Little Harriette,* or, on days when I displeased my parents, *Miss Harriette Ophelia Butlar* — I was eager to change my identity. The Lord above was to provide the perfect solution.

If only that story weren't at the county landfill now.

THE WEDDING

Harriette Ophelia Butlar
Weds
Beauregard Lee Newberry
June 24, 1967
— Headline from the Humphrey, Georgia
Banner

I was a sophomore at the University of Alabama when I met the charming, funny, and very popular Beau Newberry. We were introduced at a sorority-fraternity pledge swap. The next three years raced by as we juggled classes, football games, fraternity parties, sorority dances, and make-out sessions in the university's main library parking lot. Beau Newberry and I were married just after our graduations.

The date was selected through a lottery system, as each of my engaged sorority sisters lobbied for those all important

Saturdays in June of 1967. (We wanted to be in one another's weddings, so we drew numbers.) I secured June 24. My former roommate, Ruth Anne Oliver, stopped speaking to me and hasn't spoken to me since.

Ruth Anne, bless her heart, was divorced one year later and blamed the whole debacle on me. A noted fortune teller in Tuscaloosa had given her the third weekend of June as the perfect lining up of the moon and stars for Ruth Anne and her fiance's astrological signs. But, according to our lottery rules, Ruth Anne's wedding *had* to occur on the second weekend. Who knew?

I *am* sorry, Ruthie.

Beau and I married in the very same church in Humphrey where Mother and Daddy had married some three decades prior. It was the big event of the summer for Humphrey. Eight bridesmaids and twice as many groomsmen marched into the standing-room-only congregation. Mary Pearle, already married and, thankfully, only *slightly* pregnant at the time, served as my matron of honor. My attendants, with their tightly teased, lacquer-sprayed, helmet-like hair, wore soft green dresses with fashionable A-line skirts and short, white gloves. Each carried a bountiful bouquet of gardenias with English ivy that streamed down onto the church's floor.

The young men, tuxedo-clad and sweating profusely, performed admirably as they clearly wished for the ceremony's end. The boys were more than ready for the festivities at my parents' country club. Most of them were still trying to recover from overindulging at the rehearsal dinner party the night before.

My groom was a nervous wreck. Beau sweated more than anyone else in the church, but to me he appeared as calm, cool, and as dashingly handsome as a knight in shining armor.

As my sister had three years prior, I wore Mother's gown of antique, ivory lace. I carried peach roses and beamed as Daddy walked me down the long, green-carpeted aisle. Mother and Creola, both dressed in shades of pink, stood together on the front row and took turns weeping and making fun of one another for doing so.

Mother said our ceremony was the second most joyous day of her life, the first being her own wedding.

Creola added, "If only Miss Moonbeam and Beau weren't still such babies. I can't believe my Moonbeam's all grown."

"You look like a princess today," Daddy

whispered in my ear. My father's eyes were teary. As much as my family approved of Beau, it was obvious that none of them were ready for their last little girl to grow up.

Everything went off as planned at the church and at the reception, with the exception of minor mishaps. A waiter stumbled and dropped the sterling silver punchbowl in the center of the ballroom. Mother was horrified but also extremely relieved that none of our guests' outfits were splattered with raspberry punch. Daddy, his buddies, and Beau's fraternity brothers were elated that it was the non-alcoholic punch that got spilled.

My parents had arranged for a uniformed driver to whisk Beau and me away in grand style after the reception. We were to ride across town in Daddy's brand-new, 1967, midnight-blue Oldsmobile. We would then pick up Beau's car in the shopping center parking lot and be on our merry way to the Smoky Mountains for our honeymoon.

Beau's Chevy was there all right, exactly where he'd parked it the night before.

"Good Lord, Beau, look at *that!*" I yelled.

"Damn stupid jerks," he shouted, muttering much worse under his breath.

Beau's groomsmen had written all over his car with white paint. Their crude comments went far beyond the traditional, good-natured, *Just Married* wishes. My brain mercifully (for Beau's future relationships with these old friends) blocked out anything specific.

"Where's the nearest place we can get the car washed, Harriette?"

"Two blocks on the left. There's a gas station on the corner."

Beau gunned the engine. Moments later, the new Mr. and Mrs. Beau Newberry had resolved a good bit of our problem.

But that's not all.

Mother drove the same make and model Chevrolet as Beau's. I can only imagine her stunned reaction upon returning home to find *her* car covered with sexually specific graffiti. Seems that the pranksters, in their rush to embarrass us, managed to confuse the two automobiles. Time was of the essence, so they failed to remove the paint from Mother's car.

I always hoped the language on Mother's car was milder than on Beau's. It must have been pretty steamy, however, because, right after all the festivities were over and done with, my mother insisted that Daddy wash her car!

"And, dear, best do so in our driveway. Don't *dare* take it to the service station.

People will talk."

Daddy, still dressed in his tux, stood with garden hose in hand, wondering what kind of boy his daughter had married. He prayed sincerely that the groom was nothing like his groomsmen.

Mother never mentioned the ill-fated practical joke to me, but Daddy confronted Beau the very first chance he had. My father was still complaining to Beau about the incident up until our first child was born. But Daddy was too gentlemanly to discuss such things in front of "the girls," meaning Mother and me.

As Beau and I drove north toward Gatlinburg, Tennessee on our honeymoon, the car radio was playing *My Girl.* We sang along, "I've got sunshine on a cloudy day . . ."

Other drivers were honking and waving at us. We finally realized why.

"Guess we'd better get another carwash," grimaced Beau. "Those idiots must have used enamel!"

"Whatever you say." By then, I was too contented to care about much of anything but Beau. I smiled. "I'm your *wife.* How strange is that?"

"About as strange as me being your husband."

"We're a couple of old married folks." My

voice drifted. I admired the needlepoint purse on my lap. "Look, Beau. Can you believe I finally finished the bloomin' thing?"

I'd struggled to complete the needlepoint monogram and did so only with the able assistance of Aunts Harriette and Ophelia. God bless them. My new initials, done in yellow on a white background, were in block letters. They spelled out "H-O-N," for Harriette Ophelia Newberry.

Technically, it should have been HOBN, for Harriette Ophelia Butlar Newberry, but that simply didn't look right. "Too busy," explained the lady at the needlepoint shop. "Just use HBN." But Mother and I agreed that we couldn't offend Aunt Ophelia by leaving out her *O*. Also, it didn't matter to Daddy that I omitted the *B* for Butlar. He was far too wrapped up in the mounting wedding expenses.

"It's just a purse, darling daughter," he said. "Whatever makes my daughter and my wife happy." Always the diplomat, Daddy made that particular statement so often in April, May, and June of 1967 that he sounded like a robot.

So *HON* it was.

As we rode down the highway, Beau politely and enthusiastically made jokes over my handiwork. He proclaimed, "You're a real, *HON-ey* to me, sweetheart." He turned and quickly kissed my cheek.

I kissed him back.

"Honey, indeed. Honey Newberry."

I liked it. That was the last time anyone but my parents, Aunt Harriette, or Aunt Ophelia ever again called me *Little Harriette.*

Our first married Christmas was the only Christmas we spent apart. Beau was in Vietnam. I would never forget that night.

Beau had been oddly quiet throughout dinner that night. A great cook I wasn't just yet, but the roast beef tasted pretty good to me. Something was wrong with him, and he was obviously not ready to tell me what was going on. We went to a movie. As we sat in the theater watching Steve McQueen in *The Sand Pebbles,* Beau fidgeted, not making eye contact with me, not eating our shared popcorn, and not paying a minute's attention to the film. He continued to squeeze my hand again and again as if he were trying to resuscitate someone's heart.

Later on, Beau would admit that his initial reaction to the shock of the news was to take the afternoon off for a round of golf. He desperately needed the time to get his mind off what was happening and to figure out how to tell me about it. As a rule, he was a fine golfer, one who shot under eighty. Beau Newberry didn't break one hundred that round.

We pulled into the driveway of our small rental house. Beau put on the brake and turned to me. "I've got to go over there."

"Over where?"

"Vietnam."

It was a warm summer night, yet I was suddenly chilled to the bone. We had waited two whole years to get married because we both wanted to graduate from college first. It had only been a few short weeks since our wonderful wedding. My entire body started to tremble.

The wheels of my mind began to turn as I tried to figure out how to keep this from happening to him, to us. Pull strings? Who could we contact to get the orders changed? Perhaps the orders were wrong? Could it be a horrendous mistake? He'd enrolled in ROTC as a sound way to earn extra money for college. But Beau Newberry with orders to Vietnam? How could this be? Could I wish it away? No. Could I pray for it to disappear? I'd surely try.

"Are you certain?"

"Yes, there's no doubt about it. I got a letter. I couldn't make much sense out of the military mumbo jumbo, but a pamphlet fell out of the envelope. It read 'Familiar Vietnamese Phrases.' "

I had to laugh.

So did Beau.

Then we wept.

Beau left in six weeks.

I cried, I crumbled, I cocooned my crushed self. For days, either I couldn't eat a thing or I ate like a pig. Then I cried and I cried and I cried.

Beau was gone. I felt powerless and very, very afraid for him. His parents were terrified, too. Beau was still their baby boy. My parents, as much as they loved Beau, were as concerned for me as they were for my young husband.

Creola vowed to get back at the "Yankee" government. She was childless, and considered us her own. "I'll show them how I feel about them hurting my babies." She became a war protester, writing letter after letter to President Johnson. Creola once picketed in front of the army recruiting office in Humphrey. Her actions didn't help Beau, but it made her feel like she was doing something. I loved her for it.

I pulled myself together and landed a job as a newspaper reporter. It was interesting enough. I stayed busy. As a reporter, I was assigned to write feature stories. I also wrote about other people's weddings. I was jealous of every bride and groom. At the same time, I genuinely hoped Vietnam wouldn't separate them as it had us. I wrote letters to my second lieutenant every night. Never much of a writer before or since, Beau wrote back to me.

As the fall holidays approached I dreaded the sight of a grocery-store turkey because I saw the holiday bird as a depressing harbinger of happy times for everyone but me. I wanted to stomp Halloween pumpkins to pieces, and I knew full well that Christmas was going to be hell. I thought about carrying matches with me to set fire to anything that happened to be red, green, and festive.

On one particularly lonely afternoon in December, I came upon a woman ringing her Salvation Army bell. I dropped a dollar in her bucket. As I hurried away, my cheeks were awash with tears. The next morning, I actually walked into a street light pole while trying to avoid a store window with its ornamented tree, fake fireplace, and happy family of mannequins. *Get a grip, Honey.*

I thought about a conversation I'd had with Creola at Mother and Daddy's on the previous Sunday. After dinner, my parents were in the living room whispering something about Mary Pearle. Concerned, I walked in, but Mother quickly ushered me out.

"She's not your worry right now, dear. Everything will be fine. Besides, you have Beau to think about."

She closed the door.

"Mother?"

"Come in here," called Creola from the kitchen. "You can help me clear off the dishes."

"But, Crellie —"

"But nothing. I need you."

Creola had set a trap and I fell right in. She started with tender concern, "Precious little bride, I know you miss your Beau. Of course, you do! Just as he misses you. Miss Moonbeam, there's an old saying that goes like this, 'The days are long, but the years fly by.' I've been around long enough to know it's true."

"I hope so."

Then Creola Moon got me. As angry as she was about Beau's being in Vietnam, my *Crellie* said, "I am a little surprised at you, baby girl. And I don't quite understand." She paused as I stacked the dirty dishes and she gathered the silverware. Then Creola charged, "Feeling sorry for yourself doesn't sound one bit like the brave little girl I raised."

"I just miss him so much, Crellie." I cried as I slumped down on a dining room chair. I buried my head in my arms, and in doing so, knocked over what was left of my iced tea. "Damn!"

Mother called from the living room, "Everything all right in there?"

Creola responded, "We're doing fine. I can take care of this." She blotted the tea with a dish rag. "No harm done."

She sat down next to me. "I know, I know your heart is broken in pieces. Saw that so many times when you were little. I just wish I could fix it as easy as I did in those days."

"Me, too."

"Your Beau — *our* Beau — is coming home to us, safe and sound. I pray for him every day."

"Oh, Crellie," I threw my arms around her. "I hope you're right." How I wanted to believe her.

"Now, let's get the dessert and carry it into the living room. Best not to share our conversation. Your parents have enough on them right now."

"Tell me, Crellie. What's wrong with Mary Pearle?"

"It's that Edgar again. He's a fool. Tom-cattin' around, just like always."

"My brother-in-law thinks he's God's gift

to women!"

"That's right. God's *curse,* as I see it," she frowned. "I pray for him in the opposite way I pray for our Beau."

"Crellie!"

"Now, don't you be letting on to Mary Pearle that you know about this situation. Your sister wants everybody, especially you, to believe things are fine, especially with her baby coming."

"I'm sure the baby will bring her and Edgar together," I affirmed.

The wise Creola knew better. She said nothing, just knocked on the living room door. "All right then, who's ready for some peach pie?"

"We are!"

The four of us ate dessert as if all were right with the world.

I worried about Mary Pearle and Edgar, but as promised, I said not a word whenever Mary Pearle and I talked. Besides, despite only two years' difference, my sister still seemed so much older to me! We weren't as close then as we would become during the next few years. I confidently told Mother and Daddy that the problem would surely resolve itself.

As Creola quoted, *The days are long, but the years fly by.* I was convinced that in a year's time, we'd all be one happy family.

Creola's harsh but well intentioned words about my "Vietnam attitude" made me realize how much worse things must have been for Beau. To think, just the Christmas before, we'd gotten engaged, celebrated with our parents, with Creola, and again with our fraternity and sorority friends on New Year's Eve. Would it be cold in Bien Hoa? Probably not, just rainy. But lonely.

Beau was half a world away from me, from his family, and from everything he knew and loved. Like me and like my family, Crellie, his sister and his dear parents were also grieving themselves sick with worry. It was *Beau* who needed consolation, not his bride.

I soon started to occupy myself with helping others. Instead of weeping at the sight of a Salvation Army volunteer, I rang the bell with all my might as a volunteer for the organization. I drove to Alabama and spent more time with Beau's folks. And, in addition to my daily letters to him, I determined to start sending my husband some cheerful surprises.

One such gift turned around as a joke on me. More of a *revelation,* it was. Until that point, I'd never thought of myself as having much of a southern drawl. A friend at the newspaper let me borrow her tape recorder.

First, I practiced the mechanics of operating the machine. I then recorded a romantic and witty holiday message for Lt. Newberry.

After he listened to my gift, Beau wrote back to me: *Dear Magnolia.* I could practically hear him chuckling.

That was the *last* tape-recording from this Southern belle that the young lieutenant — and his insensitive army buddies — was to hear. Magnolia, indeed! Mad? Offended? Let's just say this Mrs. Newberry was more far comfortable with the written word, after that.

If this is a confession about my shortcomings, I must add that baking goodies had never been my long suit either. Nevertheless, I decided to send my soldier some Christmas cookies. These were to come from me and from me alone, so I stubbornly refused any assistance from Creola or from Beau's mother, Mary, a cook extraordinaire. For *Magnolia,* this was another mistake.

Oh, I baked the cookies, all right. My kitchen looked like there'd been a blizzard come through. It and I were covered in flour and butter. Tiny silver candies spilled and rolled into every nook and cranny of our house. At the end of the day, let it be written, those *darn* cookies filled two large tins and were ready for shipping. Proudly, I deposited the box at our neighborhood post office.

Two weeks later Beau wrote back. I could hear the laughter in his *ink*.

Dear Honey,

I love you. Thank you so much for the cookies. I know how hard you must have worked. They were delicious. There must have been some trouble in shipping. The guys and I had to eat them with spoons! Ha Ha.

I do love the baker with all my heart,
                                                      Beau

Dauntless, I remained single-minded in my mission to help him celebrate Christmas. As my spoken word and my attempts at baking had bombed — other than to provide a few chuckles — I decided to mail my groom a fully adorned Christmas tree. Decorating has always been my *forte*.

A trip to the corner drugstore netted the perfect three-foot fake tree. I covered it with miniature ornaments and topped it with a gold star. Stroking my engagement and wedding rings, I added sentimental messages about our previous Christmas and shared my hopes for the many, many happy holidays to come.

I carefully boxed up the tree with all matter of packing materials and took it to the post office. Giving the package to the lady behind the desk, I mentioned the disastrous results with the cookies.

"Not to worry, ma'am," she assured me. "Your package will arrive in excellent shape. Trust me; I'll see to it myself."

I walked away convinced that my tree would arrive and be the delight of Beau's barracks.

The beaten-up thing was returned to me in February. A single ornament remained unbroken, a tiny plastic Santa. A good omen of sorts, actually, because years later, Beau himself would become Santa Claus. For the last five years, he has played Santa for the children of his office workers and for those of our friends. "That little ornament was spared as a sign," Creola told me. She was right.

Beau did have a good Christmas in Vietnam. He heard from family and friends. Best of all, he got to see Bob Hope in person. The USO show was telecast. My parents, Creola, and I sat glued to the television on that December night. No, we didn't get a glimpse of Beau, but we did see the faces of many, many young soldiers just like him, who were serving their country.

On Christmas Day, I, my parents, Mary Pearle and Edgar — who'd behaved well since their baby daughter, Susan, had arrived — gathered to spend the afternoon with Beau's family and members of the Newberry clan. Yes, of course, there were tears, many tears. Yet, there was also joy in the anticipation and the absolute belief that our Beau would be safely back home with us in a few more months.

I had Daddy take my picture in front of the Newberrys' beautifully decorated Christmas tree. In the shot, I held out my empty arm indicating the exact place where Beau should have been. Thankfully, my life-sized Santa Claus returned home from Vietnam the following fall. On December 25, 1968, he and I posed in the exact same spot.

Beau was holding a plate of delicious holiday cookies, whole ones, silver candies in place, no crumbles.

He'd baked them himself.

CHAPTER 4

During that lazy morning on the beach, memories of my last birthday also drifted into mind. The event had upset me more than I cared to admit. Now, what bothered me most about the passing of another year was not my age but the fact that I had blown the short story project. I might not be good at cooking or other hobbies, but I could pride myself on an ability to weave together words. I worried about losing that knack.

Hadn't Creola let me languish long enough? When was her spirit going to tap me on the shoulder and give me some fresh advice?

Get back to work, Miss Moonbeam!

Well, that *wasn't the advice I wanted. Go away, Crellie.*

I took a sip of my drink.

Prior to leaving Atlanta for the summer, I'd announced to everyone, including my publisher, that I was done writing. *Done.* As I told Beau, our children, my sister, my friends, and anyone else who asked, "The truth is, I've said all I've got to say."

I was lying.

The reality was that I feared I didn't have another story in me.

You're on a sabbatical, I comforted myself.

I picked up the latest bestseller and began to read. Not able to concentrate, I tossed it aside without finishing the first chapter. Seeing another writer's work only made me feel guilty. The book had been a birthday present. Inside was the card from a well-meaning friend.

Happy Birthday, Honey. Bet you could write one just as good. No, yours would be much better!

Love, Pam

My friends have traditionally exhibited blind and enduring faith in me.

I recalled my last birthday, the family dinner, and the luncheon given me by my girlfriends, now a tradition, along with their painstakingly and thoughtfully selected greeting cards.

Egads, those cards with their tasteless jokes about aging! Years ago, cards with flaming cakes and bosoms cascading onto withered knees used to bring down the house at our lunches. Now those same giggling girlfriends of mine, well into our maturity, tend to purchase more *gentle* reminders of the passing years; cards with pastoral scenes, cute little animals, vows of friendship, and birds. *Birds!* Cardinals, wrens, bluebirds, robins and chickadees. Birds and the love of birds is a dead giveaway that a girl is far, far from her girlhood!

This year, Pam's card for me featured an entire *flock* of red birds.

I gulped my diet drink with the bravado of a cowboy in an old-time episode of *Gunsmoke* throwing back a hearty swig of sarsaparilla. Unlike the cowboys at Miss Kitty's saloon, however, I got choked. I spat and coughed as cola spewed from my nose. Covered with the sticky substance, I looked around to see if anyone were watching. A woman had been walking toward me, but quickly turned around and headed off in the opposite direction. I assumed she was being kind.

I waded into the surf to rinse off. It was still too early in the season for this cold-natured gal to swim, but the splashes of water refreshed me. I made footprints in the cool, wet sand as busy little sandpipers scampered around adding their miniature pricks near my feet's outlines. Securing my hat, and with the breeze at my back, I started up the beach for my daily constitutional. The Gulf glistened a brilliant gold in the morning's sunlight.

I watched the seagulls and pelicans as they windsurfed effortlessly over the water in search of prey. Spotting small fish, the birds would dive in and sail up with a tasty breakfast gripped in their bills.

"It's easy for you birds," I called. "You have no diets to observe, no meals to cook, and no dishes to wash!"

A pelican dived in for his fish.

Pelicans occupy a special place in my heart. I see them as exclusively male, strong, determined, and dependable. To me they are exactly like Beau. Though my own *pelican* is clearly more handsome than the bird variety, there was something oddly familiar in the eyes of one pelican I was able to observe up close. In the bird world, that pelican was the closest thing to the man of my life emulating his expression, his personality, his friendliness, and his resolve to eat well.

"Enjoy your morning's feast, Beau, my love!"

The sun had been up just long enough for

the heat to begin to steam. I considered turning back but urged myself to keep moving for the sake of exercise, demon exercise. In the distance, I spotted the familiar form of a woman, one who walked at the same time as me each morning.

There was nothing of a pelican's look about the woman. She reminded me more of a crane. Tall and skinny with thighs the same size as her calves, the crane-like woman almost appeared to be walking on stilts. She looked to be in her late seventies or possibly in her early eighties. Dressed in white, her gray-streaked blond hair was topped with a styrofoam safari hat. The woman was monochromatic with the exception of hot pink sunglasses.

I sighed. "Everyone is starting to look like birds to me," I told the pelicans. "Not only am I talking with birds, but I'm also comparing other humans to water fowl. I'd best initiate some human contact, and soon!"

Following traditional beach etiquette, the woman and I had begun by nodding greetings to each other for a couple of weeks. Our polite nods next became hearty "Good mornings!" and had now progressed to the point where I actively looked for her each day.

This day something else happened. The

birdlike walker stopped some fifty feet down the beach and turned a cartwheel. For a split second, I feared she had taken a fall. I rushed to her aid.

She sprang to her feet and threw her arms in the air as if she'd scored a touchdown. "I have grand and marvelous news on this glorious morning!"

I halted, looking around to see if this rather strange exhibition had been for another person. No, the large bird was definitely performing for *me.* Now rethinking my tendency to be friendly, I cautiously approached her.

"Are you all right? I was concerned you might be hurt."

"What? Me hurt? For heaven's sake, I'd never allow for such a thing. I'm the very picture of grace!"

"Apparently so."

"Should I assume that *you* don't turn cartwheels when life is being especially good to you?"

"Actually, no. No, I don't."

"And why not?"

"Because I can't?" My voice rose on *can't* as if I were asking the woman's permission to confess my inability.

"For goodness sakes, I'll teach you. It's rather simple." With that, she turned three more cartwheels.

I applauded. "So, tell me, what is this remarkable news?"

"My dear, you can't escape so easily. My announcement must be delayed because I'm on a mission. Charming beachcomber, I must instruct you in elementary gymnastics, first."

"Thank you, but it's not gonna happen. Trust me."

I had a flashback to elementary school gym class where I suffered humiliating defeat as my body failed to flip, twist, turn, or perform any skill beyond a front somersault.

The woman frowned in frustration. Her intense look of disappointment made me think of Creola.

I stood at attention. "Okay, but you'd best step back or you might get hurt." I gingerly put my hands palms down on the sand. Kicking like a mule, I threw my feet up into the air and came down on my back with a resounding thud.

The stranger bent over me. "A fine first effort!"

"Oh, you think so, do you? I'm just glad I didn't break my neck." I looked around for a jeering audience. The beach was mostly unpeopled. For that mercy, I was abundantly thankful.

"Try again, but this time, I'm going to help you. Here, give me your feet."

Determined more than self-conscious, I staggered upright, bent over, placed my hands in the sand, and raised my feet, one at a time. The woman gripped me by the ankles and shoved. "All right, over you go!"

Indeed, over I went. It was my first cartwheel in a half century of humiliating efforts. I shouted and cheered as if I'd won Olympic gold. "Did you see *that?*"

"Yes! How graceful you were!"

"My lord, is anybody else looking?"

"And what difference would that make? As a matter of fact, an accomplishment is all the finer *with* an audience!"

"You know, you're right."

Like old friends, the two of us strolled up the beach together. The wind was in our faces. A cool breeze energized me.

"I do feel rather silly."

"My dear, you must get over that. Life is far too short to worry about whether or not you're being silly." She paused. "Ah hah, methinks it's more what *other* people think that concerns you?"

"Not really. Well, maybe so."

"The truth is, we all might get a great deal more accomplished were we to act as suited ourselves. That is, as long as we stay within the laws of common civility." She added, "If we must!"

"You make it sound so simple."

"Listen to me, my young friend, and you'll learn to get more out of life. I'll guide you from my own rather lengthy experience."

"All right, then. Do you practice what you preach?"

"There is no other path for me. Now, when are you going to ask me about my show of jubilation?"

"This very minute. I'm afraid I got caught up with my cartwheel, *our* cartwheel. Enough! Please tell me your news."

"My son, Jennings, called this morning, and he's coming for the weekend! The darling boy works so hard he hasn't a moment to spare. Naturally, his phone call merited my joyous display."

"Naturally!"

"Now, tell me about *your* children. I see you're a mother, too."

"You can *see* that? It's because I'm out of shape, isn't it?"

"What are you talking about? Your shape is fine. I believe you could use a self-confidence tune-up!"

I felt my face heating from embarrassment. This total stranger seemed to look inside me. I wasn't sure I liked that. I'd once consulted a psychiatrist when I was trying to deal with the stresses of caring for aging parents. Even with a professional sleuth seated across from me, I'd managed to maintain my optimistic and controlled southern persona. My consuming fear for our parents' plight remained comfortably imprisoned behind my smiling and hopeful mask. No, I wasn't about to open up to this lady, either.

She peered harder at me. "I only deduced that you're a mother because of the way you watch after people, specifically the way you watch after children on this beach. You see, I'm a skilled observer of humanity. I don't merely walk on the beach, I take notice of what's going on. I've noticed how you keep an eye out for others. Yesterday, I watched you run into the water after a child's lost bucket. Such actions demonstrate your concern."

"My, but you are observant. Yes, you're right. I was worried about the toddler. He was ready to chase his bucket right into the water. I could see his mother was preoccupied with her younger child."

"My point exactly."

"I've noticed you, too. You and I walk at the same time every day."

"Kindred spirits, dear, we are of kindred spirits."

My embarrassment faded and I began to feel invigorated. Although she appeared much older than me, my new acquaintance was amazingly youthful. What a perceptive mind she had. And such a positive attitude! A good attitude is such an important quality; what's more, her spunk was beginning to rub off on me. Hadn't I just turned my first cartwheel? And this with the help of someone who was at least twenty years my senior!

"Where does your son live?" I asked.

"Oh, Jennings, such a precious boy! My Jennings lives in Atlanta. He works for a large company there. But I must confide that his heart is really in the arts. He just cannot discover a way to liberate himself from the corporate world. His real vocation is in writing. I say never fear, for Jennings is young, not yet forty."

"Young. Not yet forty." I suddenly felt younger. The crane woman was like a fresh breeze.

"What do you do, young lady?"

I didn't want to admit what I did because of the inevitable next question, "What do you write?" Which was often followed with, "Are you writing something now?" I wanted to nip that in the bud so I replied, "I'm simply on vacation and enjoying every minute of it. I feel so rejuvenated by the beach. Sometimes I return just to fill my lungs with salt air. The first time I step onto the sand, particularly after a long winter away, I feel plugged into some sort of energy. Weird, don't you think?"

The woman cut her eyes at me. "One must feed one's soul, especially if one is creative. We are all creators in one way or another."

Her message was unmistakable.

Had this casual meeting had been arranged by the spirit of Creola Moon? Crellie had always been a wise old owl to me. I almost wanted to cup my ear and listen for a *wwwhooooo* from amongst the nearby palm trees. That feisty owl was somewhere nearby. For certain. I could feel her presence.

"You remind of someone," I said.

My walking companion smiled at me. "Like you, I too am best fed by the salt air and sea."

I found myself trying to pinpoint her curious accent. It had the flavor of an English person's, yet it was also not anything I readily recognized. I only knew she was not from the South. I nearly bit a hole in my tongue when I heard myself inquire, "So, where are you from?"

How Southern was that?

"My dear, I'm from the Continent by birth, but I am currently from *Every Place*." She mouthed the words as if *every place* were her country. "I'm neither fish nor am I fowl. I am happy at sea or on the land. I'm at home anywhere I am home. And you, dear, where is home for you?"

Wishing to appear somewhat worldly to her, this Georgia native replied, "Well, ma'am, for the entire summer, my home is right here on this beach." I immediately wanted to swallow back the "ma'am" word. *Ma'am* was certain to expose my country origins.

"And your name, dear, what's your name?"

"I'm Harriette. Harriette Newberry." Harriette? What was I trying to keep from the woman? "And yours?"

"Now there's a thought provoking query for *you,* because I have numerous names. To some, I am Beatrice, to others, simply Bea. There are those among my dear ones who call me Aunt Beattie, or Madame B. I decree that you must choose your own name for me."

"I like Beatrice. It was the first you mentioned. In my opinion, it becomes you." I wondered why the lady hadn't shared her last name. Who was I to question? Hadn't I just given the woman an alias?

"That's fine, dear, but do pronounce my name like thus, *Be-AT-trice.* Please put the accent on the 'at.' "

"*Be-AT-trice.* I'll practice. Beatrice, Beatrice, Beatrice!"

"Very good, Harriette. You are doing the name its justice!"

"Thank you very much," I said with flourish.

"But, my young friend, I must bid you a very good day. So farewell, for the present, darling Harriette."

I was disappointed that our conversation ended so abruptly, but I politely bid goodbye. Actually I said, "Bye-bye now." I bit my tongue. How Southern can you get?

We traded a wave as I walked in the direction of the condo. I was glad I'd finally introduced myself to the eccentric beachcomber. What an *encourager* was Beatrice! I would scratch from my *To Do* list the formerly unlikely accomplishment of *Learn to turn a cartwheel.*

Did you make a note of that, Creola? A cartwheel! I know you were watching.

I again lamented the fact that I'd not been

named for my elegant Aunt Mary Pearle
Butlar Armstrong.

Drat, did I really say, "Bye-bye?"

CHAPTER 5

I inhaled the fresh ocean air and, settling back into my beach chair, took a sip of my un-iced, all-but-boiling diet drink. At least, no bee had fallen into the can. I'd swallowed one once, at the beach. I was very thirsty, too much so to go upstairs for ice. The bee-less drink suited me fine.

Moonbeam, why on earth did you give Beatrice your old name? Even worse, why didn't you tell her you were an author?

Were? I thought. Curious. My work in past tense? I pulled my hat down over eyes to hide from my own negative thoughts. *Go away, Crellie. I'm resting.*

The sun sparkled through the holes in my straw hat. I closed first one eye then the other, playing a game of illusion that my hat was moving back and forth. At an angle through the tiny holes, I could see the sun, a passing cloud, a flock of birds. It was intriguing, what simple pleasures a person could experience when away from the phone, the computer, and the demands of busy days.

As if on cue, my cell phone rang. "Oh, hello, Beau. What's going on?"

He was busy at work, everything was fine at home, and by the way, he did have some news. Not good.

"Oh, no! Are you sure you have to cancel? I was sooooo looking forward to your being down here."

After hearing my disappointment, Beau promised he'd come the following weekend.

"Cross your heart and hope to die?"

"That sounds threatening," growled my husband. "Tell you what, for good measure, I'll tack on Monday as a bonus."

"It's a deal, and you don't have to cross your heart. Oh, Beau, guess what?" I didn't expect any guesses from him. I knew my husband wasn't much for playing guessing games, especially when calling from his office. "The woman of your dreams actually turned her first cartwheel!"

"Uh, that's nice. There goes my other line. I gotta go." It's not unusual for Beau to skirt over such an announcement.

"I said a *cartwheel,* Beau Newberry." I stood up as if he could see me. "I learned how to turn a cartwheel!"

"Didn't know that was a big priority of yours."

My husband was the poster person for the typical man. I could forgive him for that. I'd learned to be accepting of his obvious flaws, and he of mine. Besides, since my hysterectomy a few years earlier, I had not been nearly as sweet-natured. Beau had made admirable adjustments. It had been at least three years since he'd pushed my buttons by asking, "What's wrong with you, sweetheart? Do you need your hormones?"

Saying goodbye, I eased myself back into the chair and continued to watch the world go by through the holes in my straw hat. The sounds of the gentle, rolling waves carried me back in time.

Another of my short stories refused to evaporate into the ether.

CREOLA AT THE BEACH

BY HONEY NEWBERRY

It was 1952, and our family was vacationing at the beach. Mother and Daddy, Mary Pearle and I held hands and ran, squealing, into the Gulf. We played for hours before wolfing down a picnic lunch of bologna and cheese sandwiches, soggy potato chips, lemonade, and homemade peanut butter cookies. Food always tastes better near water.

The only negative thing about our annual two-week trips to the beach was that Creola could never go along with us. Year after year, she insisted that she couldn't be away from her own family for so long. That wasn't altogether true, but I wouldn't understand why for some time.

Creola would tell wonderful stories — scary ones — as well as stories that made her Moonbeam and Priceless Pearlie laugh so hard we'd roll backwards and often right off our seats. More than once, as a child, I had to change my clothes because I wet my pants laughing.

Creola didn't mind washing my pants, so she said. She'd declare that the wetting of my things was her responsibility in the first place. "I made you laugh too hard, child!"

Even so, she expected me to assist her in the task. I especially liked when Creola lifted me up to hang things on the outdoor clothes line. I would take the wooden clothespins from my teeth and carefully secure them on either end of each piece of laundry.

Once the sheets and towels and all the clothes were hung securely on the line, Creola, Mary Pearle, and I would run through the billowing material. I'd pretend to be aboard a ship just off the coast of some far, exotic island. I was the vessel's captain, with Crellie and Priceless Pearlie as my crew. The best part was when we danced about among the "sails."

Mother vehemently disapproved of our nanny's telling us ghost stories, some of which were tinged with the voodoo tales of her native New Orleans. Creola regularly promised Mother that she'd stick to lighter subject matter, and I think she honestly meant to. "I surely don't want to frighten my darlin' girls, Missus. You know how I love these babies."

When we pleaded and pleaded, our soft-hearted nanny would often give in once our mother went out for a day of bridge. We had to promise Creola we'd have no bad dreams. For good balance, at the end of a particularly terrifying tale Creola would tell us a *funny* story. We sisters not only needed one to counteract our fright, but also as something that we could share at the dinner table to the appreciative audience of Mother and Daddy.

"Miss Moonbeam, Priceless Pearlie," moaned a dramatic Creola one rainy afternoon. Her hands extended, her eyes dilated to solid black with the full whites showing. "That evil ghost is coming up our basement steps all the way from the back of our loud, loud fire-breathing furnace. He gonna eat us up alive!"

"Oh, Creola," we yipped in unison, then snuggled as close as we could to her on the living room couch. "Hold us tight!"

"Now, darling children, you know how your sweet mother — may The Angel of Good Luck bless her bridge game — feels about our ghosts. I dare not scare my baby girls on this dark, most stormy day."

"Crellie, I'm not scared, not one bit. I'm almost seven, you know!"

"And I'm already nine," puffed up Mary Pearle, "so you know I can take it!"

Creola took a deep, heavy breath. "Listen, do you sweet little ladies hear something?"

"No, s-s-surely not, Creola," I stammered.

"Yes, I do!" said my sister.

She tapped her foot. "That ghost is walking closer to us, babies!"

"Oh, Crellie!" We screamed as we dove under a pair of throw pillows and just missed cracking open our heads on one another.

"Lord have mercy, my babies, are you hurt?" She cradled us. "Your mother is right. It's best that your old Creola not say one word more!"

"Oh, Crellie, please keep telling us!"

"Pleeeeaassse!"

Sighing, she gave in. "Well, get yourselves ready, because he's coming closer, and closer, and closer, *stomp, stomp,* and closer, *stomp.*"

I wanted to squeeze myself under a seat cushion. Yet, shaking as I was, I knew full well this was the most fun in the whole world.

"Closer and closer, *stomp, stomp.*"

"Crellie." I couldn't let out a breath.

Mary Pearle squealed and put another throw pillow over her head.

Creola grabbed us and shouted to the ceiling, "Gotcha!"

Mary Pearle screamed like a banshee. I jumped off the couch and screamed, too, as I ran in circles around our living room. Creola picked me up and, collapsing back on the couch, we laughed and laughed. Had it been a sunny day, even Creola's clothes would have been on the line drying when Mother got home from bridge.

That night, over Creola's fried chicken, the story we shared with Mother and Daddy was about Creola's ninety-year-old father and his new hat.

As usual, I insisted on telling it.

"Mother and Daddy, it goes like this. A dirty old hobo came by the Moons' house. He was asking for a handout. So Creola's mother gave the man a brand new hat, one with a bright, red feather. The trouble was that the hat belonged to Creola's father. Worse, he'd only had it for a week! Later that evening, Creola's father was sitting out on the front porch whittling on his wood pipe. Here came that old hobo man strutting down the middle of the street. He stopped and tipped his hat at Mr. Moon, proud as you please.

"Creola's father looked up. He kind of squinted and said, 'Say, feller, where'd you get that fine hat?' "

Mary Pearle started to giggle, and I could hardly get out the words, but I kept on with my telling.

"The hobo said, 'Don't rightly know what to say, Mister. Reckon as you should ask your missus about my hat.'

"The man just took off running. Creola's father tossed down his whittling and stomped back inside the house."

I took a gulp of milk.

"Best slow down, sweetheart," urged Daddy. "We've got all evening to hear your story."

"Yes sir, I know." I wiped my mouth with my napkin and kept going. "Creola says her father is scared to death of her mother because, because —" I was so tickled I could hardly say what came next — "because Mrs. Moon is two times bigger than Mr. Moon!" I was hysterical. "And so . . ." I stood up in the seat of my chair for dramatic effect.

"Be careful, Little Harriette!" Mother warned.

"Yes, ma'am. Where was I? Oh, yes. Creola's father took a long look at the frown on his big ol' wife's face, and he never once said another word about that hat!"

Mother smiled and patted Daddy's hand.

"You see, darling, Creola has paid attention to us. She's no longer filling our daughters' heads full of those dreadful ghost stories."

With that, Mary Pearle and I slid under the table, laughing.

Mother lifted the tablecloth. "Girls?"

Daddy, who didn't worry nearly as much about Creola's ghost stories, changed the subject. "Dear, where did you put my favorite sweater? I can't find that old thing anywhere."

Mother, likely more open-minded than she appeared to be, replied primly, "Well, sweetheart, perhaps you should look for that nasty, moth-eaten thing on the back of Creola's hobo."

I counted the years since Mary Pearle and I lost our parents. Was it four, or five years? No, it was coming up on six. There were days when it felt still longer. Mother cared for Daddy with such dedication that she was worn to a frazzle by the time he passed away. She joined her beloved less than three months later.

At Mother's funeral, Creola engulfed me in her arms as if I were still a child.

"Miss Moonbeam! My heart is all but cracked in two."

I hugged her tightly. "Oh, Crellie, I'm glad you're here." She looked so different, so much older. How long had it been? Even though we talked on the phone from time to time and always during the holidays, it had been at least a year since I'd seen Creola in person. How could life have become too busy for me to visit this dear woman?

Even so, Creola judged me not. And on that mournful day, she comforted her Moonbeam as if I was no longer a grown woman, a wife or a mother. Because of Creola, I could briefly return to being a distressed little girl who was being reassured by someone who loved her dearly.

"Mrs. Butlar was such a fine, fine lady. Lord above, how proud she was of you! I'll miss her and miss your father every day the good Lord gives me to live. Even though I retired many years ago, your Mother still checked on me every week until she got so sick herself."

A pang of guilt hit me.

Images of Mother and Creola talking at the kitchen table washed into my mind's eye. In the end, Creola and Mother had become caregivers for one another.

Stooped and aged markedly, Creola leaned heavily on me. "I'd have been there for Mr. Butlar's service, but I was ailing on my own."

I took her arm. "Crellie, what's wrong

with you?"

"Not one thing, Sugar. I've just had one of those short-time virus bugs. Bug or no, I had to be with you today. Now that your father *and* your mother have gone to Heaven, you need your Crellie all the more."

I could barely hold back my tears. "I'm not really an orphan, am I?"

"Not as long as I have the strength to be here with you. Afterwards, I'll watch over you from the closest cloud I can find. Or maybe I'll fly down and perch on a tree branch."

"I do love you, Crellie."

"I love you, too, child."

"Let's find us a quiet place to sit in this funeral-parlor crowd. There, Miss Moonbeam, I see one over in the corner." The two of us settled comfortably onto a loveseat.

"How's Beau? How's your children? But first, tell me about you. Lord, but it's good to see Creola's Moonbeam!"

I obeyed her and did a tiny bit of bragging about my work. She beamed as I filled her in on her "grandbabies," Mary Catherine and Butlar. She laughed about Beau's latest antics on the golf course. From day one, Creola had liked my husband far more than she liked Mary Pearle's. Fact was, she couldn't stand Edgar from the day Mary Pearle brought him home to meet the family.

Creola had a second sense about the fellow. Like a cat perceives an evil presence, she saw through him well before any of us did. She huffed and puffed and only begrudgingly put out some store-bought cookies for him. On a paper plate.

When Beau came home from college with me the first time, Creola baked her exceptional lemon pound cake and winked at him as she served it, offering him as much as he could eat. She used Mother's best china and sterling silver forks.

At our wedding, Creola sat proudly in the first row with Mother and Daddy. But at Edgar and Mary Pearle's she chose the back row of the church, where she positioned herself with arms folded, eyes cast downward. Her only expression was a judging scowl. Afterwards, she embraced her Priceless Pearlie and whispered gently and sincerely in her ear, "Remember darling child, you can always come home to your Crellie."

Sitting there at the funeral parlor with her, I sighed, remembering. "Crellie, I am feeling so *old* now that Mary Catherine and Butlar are rarely at home. They're busy with their own lives. Beau and I get left in their dust. Before we can turn around, our children will be gone for good."

"As they should. You and your sister grew up too fast for me, too. Life sneaks up on us; it has a way of passing, fast as lightening."

"You told me that a long, long time ago. Remember when Beau was in Vietnam and you said 'The days are long, but the years fly by'? These days, I certainly understand that gem of your advice."

Creola smiled. "It's the truth. Before you know it, you have an empty nest."

"I don't want an empty nest. Crellie, I really think this empty nest business *is for the birds!*"

"Baby girl, you and Beau are still just children to me. You best be looking forward to many happy times in that pretty nest of yours."

I hugged her. "You've always known exactly what to say to me."

Creola, not one to enjoy a compliment, changed the subject. "I really liked your last book. You're a funny lady, yes, you are. And, my gracious goodness, how you can tell a story!"

"You must know who taught me, don't you, Crellie?"

"Who, Miss Moonbeam?"

"You!"

With that she squeezed my hands. "I'm pleased and proud you learned something good from me."

I stroked Creola's gnarled fingers, fingers so badly crippled from arthritis. Years of hard work had taken a dreadful toll. I could only imagine the pain that continued to twist Creola's bones. I also felt the softness of her hands. Like Creola herself, all the pain she had endured was camouflaged in her smooth, velvety skin. "Crellie, let me help you —"

"Help me do what? Hush, now. I best go hug Priceless Pearlie or she'll be getting jealous of us two."

"Mary Pearle always insisted you liked me best."

"Lord have mercy! Do you think that's true?"

"Sure, I do."

"Ummm humm."

As Creola walked away, the sun caught her hair and turned her solid white curls into a bright and shining halo.

Not long after, Creola moved into a retirement home. I went to see her. We visited a while, then she put both hands on her walker and stood. "I'm glad you came, my darling Moonbeam, but I must hug you and scoot. You see, I'm just like Mary Catherine and Butlar. I'm as busy as a bee. It's time for my painting class!"

I laughed. "Crellie, you're never still!"

"I got to keep my nest from getting empty. You do the same now, you hear?"

As at Mother's funeral, she passed a large window and the sun once again proclaimed Creola Moon's sainthood. Not long after, she died.

CHAPTER 6

I sat in my beach chair, crying. I gathered my things and went back up to the condo. I called my sister. Her answer machine came on.

"You'd better call me back soon, Priceless Pearlie. I've been thinking about the good old days and am about to dive into a box of animal crackers."

"My goodness, animal crackers, Honey? Your voice sounds strange. Now, 'fess up, little sister. You're grazing on junk food, so I know good and well something's wrong."

"Nothing's wrong. I'm just bored, I guess. I started thinking about Mother and Daddy and about Crellie. She always loved to give us chocolate milk and animal crackers. I need a Priceless Pearlie fix, that's all. You should jump on a plane. Cookies and milk will be waiting for you."

"Served in your little blue tea set?"

"Nope, the tea set is in my china cabinet

in Atlanta."

"Well, I'm not coming then! Seriously, I *will* be there soon. I do need to talk with you about something, something important."

"You do?"

"Yes, but it can wait."

"Come on, it's absolutely gorgeous down here. Besides, Beau's not coming until next weekend." With that, I held the phone over the deck's rail so my sister could hear the waves.

"Don't tempt me, Harriette Ophelia, you know I've got Susan's wedding coming up. I'll see you then."

"Of course! I wouldn't miss my own niece's wedding. But don't you need a little beach break *before* the wedding?"

"Now, now, I'll see you there, then we'll go back to the beach, together."

Mary Pearle and I talked for an hour or more. Through the years, we had become the closest, the dearest of friends. Even so, my sister remained evasive about the *something* she wanted to tell me. Naturally, all of her thoughts were revolving around her daughter's wedding. Like the current trend in nuptial extravagances, the ceremony and reception to follow had taken on the details and the stress of the making of a major motion picture.

"Enough about that," said Mary Pearle. "Now, tell me about your creative self. Is that computer on fire?"

My cell phone beeped. I checked the screen. "I'll call you right back. It's Mary Catherine."

"Tell her hello from her favorite aunt."

I chatted with my daughter, then called Mary Pearle back. "Mary Catherine was just checking in. My sweet daughter didn't even ask for money, this time. I think she's finally growing up. Oh, she said to tell Aunt Mary Pearle that the fitting for the bridesmaid dress went great. In fact, she actually *likes* the dress, and loves the champagne color. Okay, so let's get back to *that* topic, the wedding, of course."

"Oh, I see. It seems you still aren't writing. I can always tell when you are avoiding my encouragement."

"*Et tu, Brute?* Why can't anyone understand that I'm simply not interested in working during my vacation?"

"Whoops, I must have hit a nerve. Sorry, sister, case closed. So what else is going on?"

I told her about Beatrice. "Can you stand it? I finally learned how to turn a cartwheel? Who said you can't teach an old dog new tricks!"

"I could have a field day with that remark," threatened Mary Pearle. "Suffice to say, you can reward yourself with a glass of wine instead of a dog biscuit!"

"Okay, okay, very funny. Seriously, there is something about Beatrice that reminds me of Mother and Crellie. It's that look in the woman's eyes. You remember, that look Mother or Crellie gave us when they knew something was going on but were waiting for us to confess?"

"*That* look," sighed Mary Pearle. "Oh, yes. I do miss them so much."

"I miss *both* our mothers. Sometimes, I used to think Mother was yours and Crellie was mine!"

"Ah hah, so you finally admit that Creola was partial to you!"

"You had Mother."

"Yes, but Creola was more fun."

"Well, *nani nani, boo boo!* You and I can't even talk on the phone without arguing like children!"

"Restores our youth, don't you think? And that, sister dear, is a very good thing."

"Seriously, Mary Pearle, it was really Daddy I sometimes worry about. The poor man was the fifth wheel in a family of all females. He probably needed someone else around, another guy."

"Of course, he did, don't you know that's why he always encouraged us to choose male dogs as pets?" Mary Pearle laughed at her own wry comment, then her mood abruptly changed. "Honey, you know something? To this day, I will still pick up the phone to ask Mother a question."

"I know. I do the same thing. Thank goodness we can call each other." As I often do when not wanting to deal with the sad things in life, I made light of the situation. I moaned dramatically, "My phone bill can surely attest to that!"

"It's only money. Speaking of our childhoods, Honey, you do understand that we two are the exception to the rule in this day of 'dysfunction?' "

"You're right. Our growing-up years were perfect compared to most people's. Maybe that's why you've had such a hard time with your divorce? Seriously."

"Could be. I always assumed that my marriage would be as happy as our parents'. Miss 'Formerly Perfect Pearlie' certainly blew her mission."

"Lest we forget that our own Crellie warned you time and time again that Edgar was something of a tomcat?"

"I should have paid attention to her. To

Daddy's opinion of him, too, for that matter."

"Maybe so, Mary Pearle, but who's to know for sure? I remember how handsome Edgar was, and how romantic."

"Prince Charming lost his crown."

"I can tell you exactly what my former brother-in-law could do with that crown when he finds it!"

"Now, now, Honey."

"Mary Pearle, from the very beginning, that sorry man was ninety-eight percent of the problem in your marriage. You did more than your part to keep things together. That observation, darling sister, is from my totally objective point of view." My sister listened but made no comment. I continued, "Hey, lady, look on the bright side. You *do* have two wonderful daughters to show for your efforts."

"Thank you, Miss Moonbeam. You've always been the more positive of the Butlar girls. I love you for that."

"I love you, too, but listen, lady, Beau is going to give me his cell phone lecture if I stay on much longer. Tell you what, let's talk on Sunday afternoon. Will you be home?"

"We'll be up to our elbows addressing the wedding invitations, and it would be lovely to have a break. Wait, I may be going out to dinner, so call me early."

"Out to dinner? With whom? Susan?"

"Ask me no questions, I'll tell you no lies! Bye, for now."

"Wait!"

"Gotta go. Love you!"

After my sister hung up her telephone, I stood holding mine and wondering what she was keeping from me. Curious, it wasn't like her to be so evasive. I finally dismissed the thought. My sister was overwhelmed with Susan's wedding and had a million things on her mind.

Pouring a glass of wine, I went out on the condo's balcony. Thus far, I'd made the most of my break. I'd enjoyed much-needed quiet time, alone. Meeting Beatrice had proven to be a blessing. What had she said? That creative people need to be fed? Beatrice was a stranger, yet intuitive about my needs, and she was right on target.

My mind flipping about, I wished Beau were with me.

Our favorite area restaurant is adjacent to the local marina. I'm not sure it has an actual name. Beau always calls it "The Hole in the Wharf." A quaint, rickety-porched place filled with locals, it is legendary for shrimp and oysters. We always sat at an old, whitewashed picnic table topped with red and white checkered oilcloth, set with a candle that flickered in the water's breeze. The two of us would talk and peel fresh, boiled shrimp as we watched fishing boats dock and unload their day's catch.

It was there I first spotted the pelican that looked like Beau. Once, when I went to the restaurant alone, the friendly bird paddled around and around the marina as if to make a promise to me: *Just to let you know, Honey, I'll be here to watch out for you while he's back home in Georgia!*

Even when Beau couldn't come to the beach with me, I felt comfortable and safe. I liked the condo, mostly because of its view. I delighted in the gorgeous vistas of water and the magnificent sunsets. I loved the sounds of waves crashing beneath the bedroom window. How gently the waves lulled me to sleep each night. I could even justify the scrumptious meals of seafood; almost guiltless was I because I could counter the calories with swims in the condo pool and long walks by the water.

But it was time for me to get something accomplished. I decided to go to the grocery store. I was out of everything. I parked my car, grabbed a buggy, and began to gather fresh produce. I noticed a boy who looked oddly familiar to me. He was staring at me, just as I stared at him. How strange. I felt as if I'd known him from some place. It felt like an *uncomfortable* place. *Get a grip, Honey, he's just a kid.*

The boy began to poke at his mother, who was intensely reading the labels on frozen diet meals. His mother was my kind of cook.

I figured that I must have seen them around the beachside community and that's why her son seemed familiar. Yet I still couldn't shake my feeling of dread as I looked at the boy. Harry Potter, he looked like Harry Potter. With shock, I remembered. *That's the kid from the middle school!*

I ducked around the frozen food aisle. It was too late.

Here came his mother. "Mrs. Newberry, please forgive the interruption, but my son has talked so much about you and your visit to his school. You know, his school in Atlanta. Henry tells me you are down here writing your new novel."

"Yes, and I really must be getting back to work," I said sheepishly. Another lie. I had hit an all time low. Not only was I lying to schoolchildren, but I was also lying to their mothers.

"My son is not the only member of our family who is a fan of your work. I've read several of your books, Mrs. Newberry, the ones geared more for adults."

"That's lovely to know. Thank you."

"Why yes, in fact, my book club has reviewed your novels. We girls always identify with you, and I, for one, love the way you make us find humor in the most human of things, particularly concerning our families."

"Oh, dear."

"Yes, indeed. Doesn't everyone have an eccentric aunt? You make us feel, well almost normal!"

"I wish I felt normal."

"We don't mean to keep you, but there is just one more thing. Henry, here, is something of a writer himself. Perhaps you would enjoy reading some of his work?" Before I could utter a single word, she went on, "In fact, Henry, go out to the van right this minute and gather up your theme papers. I'll chat with Mrs. Newberry while we wait."

Henry wouldn't budge.

Good boy.

"Henry? Go on, dear," warbled the mother, as she attempted to push her son from behind. "Oh dear, you know how children can be. Henry is a bit shy, you understand." Ever hopeful, the woman raised her chin, and, pointing her eyes toward the parking lot, she urged him with her head.

He didn't yield.

Thank goodness.

I jumped in. "Yes, of course, I understand. I have two grown children. It really might be a good idea to let Henry share his work in his own good time."

"Perhaps you're right." By then, she was frowning at the boy.

I wanted to embrace the young man with gratitude, but decided it was best not to give away my relief at being let off the hook. Reading theme papers was not my favorite form of recreation.

"Mrs. Newberry, my son and I do wish you the best of luck on your next book. We'll both look forward to reading it."

The boy piped up. "Are you coming to my school, again?"

"If I'm invited," I chirped. *He likely wants another free period; anything but algebra.*

I felt like the biggest fraud. I thanked the endearing mother but couldn't look her straight in the eyes. Henry extended his hand. His long, dark eyelashes swept the back of his glasses.

What a nice kid he is, I concluded. I, on the other hand, was an absolute jerk.

His mother sighed. "Thank you for your

offer to read Henry's work. Maybe he'll be more enthused when next we meet."

"I'm sure he will be."

As I hurriedly gathered groceries and pushed my cart to the check-out line, I felt lower than dirt. First a liar, now a hypocrite. I reviewed our conversation in my mind. Should I have explained to the mother and son that I simply have very little to say *just now?* Nothing is worse than writing simply because you think you should. Yes, that's what I should have said. I could have sounded lofty and profound.

Why is it that one always thinks of a perfect response five minutes after the opportunity passes?

I loaded my supplies in my car and drove from the parking lot.

The truth was, it was well past time for me to get back to writing, if for no other reason than to please Henry and his mother. A sudden clap of thunder rallied my attention. *Drat,* it was looking as if I would be stuck inside the condo for awhile. Or was God Himself now speaking to me? Was He sentencing Honey Newberry to a writer's prison? Perhaps He was. For whatever reason — the Lord, Henry and his mother, Beau's absence, Beatrice, or my sister's prodding, I decided to pay heed.

Creola, I hope you're pleased, too.

I opened the closet door. Somewhere between the extra towels and my just-in-case winter sweater, I reluctantly dug for my laptop. Found! I plugged it in. The blue screen came into focus. Admittedly, there was something exhilarating about my computer's booting up.

I opened my files. "Short Stories.doc" jumped out at me. Here were some stories I'd never quite finished. They might end up in the landfill, too, but I might as well give them a chance.

Go on, Moonbeam, work on that story.

All right, Crellie, all right.

I began to type.

ROOFERS FROM HELL

BY HONEY NEWBERRY

We needed to put a new roof on the house. Immediately. I could tell that from my vantage point in the middle of our bed. Beau was in Chicago on a business trip. It was close to midnight and I was holding an umbrella in one hand and the telephone book in the other. Rain soaked our comforter. I balanced the umbrella's handle with my chin and shoulder as I fumbled to put on my glasses. *Roofing contractors.* I dialed.

The roofers arrived two days later. The crew was made up of one of the most outrageous bands of people I had ever encountered. They didn't just arrive, no; they rolled in like a gargantuan human tumbleweed. Their pickup truck looked as if it may have turned over a few times on the way to our house.

Don't be judgmental, Moonbeam.

They headed my way.

One tattooed, bearded beast with a well-cultivated beer belly burped with every step he took. Another was stick-skinny. His fingers were magnetically drawn — almost in a rhythm — from his nose to his groin and back to his nose. I wondered how he'd manage to free his hands long enough to nail the shingles.

A third was neither man nor woman. Its face was pointed toward mine. Was it ogling me? I couldn't decide. One eye faced east, the other west.

More judgmental stuff. Just quit.

Then I saw the most curious person in the group. He was a small ragamuffin of a boy with a mop of carrot-red hair. He leapt out from the cab of the truck. He picked his nose with the enthusiasm of the thin man. Ah hah, I figured, those two were related. I worried that the boy would ultimately turn into one of these frightful men. Inevitable. Sad.

I watched through the kitchen window as the crew prepared to start the job. Shingles, black gunk, hammers, and boxes of nails were unloaded. Experience told me that this project was going to make a major mess.

I couldn't get my mind off the little boy. It was quite early on Saturday morning. Our children were sleeping comfortably in their beds. There was this little guy being dragged along with those horrible men. He was destined to sit in the increasingly hotter sun — all day long. Oh, my heart.

I awakened our children. "Come on guys. We're going out for breakfast!"

"Oh boy!"

"Mom, what's all that racket?" asked Mary Catherine.

"Just the roofers. This is going to be a noisy day." I started to explain that this meant it wouldn't be raining in Mom and Dad's room anymore, but that wasn't much of an issue for grade-schoolers. However, I did say, "I'm going to invite someone to come along with us."

"A roofer man! Great! Can I climb up on top of the house and watch him work when we get back?" pleaded Butlar.

"No! No climbing on the roof! And, it's not an adult who may go with us. It's a little boy. He must be eight or so. He's with the roofers. I think the little guy deserves a treat." I tried to encourage the children to reach out in kindness to other people.

Butlar looked concerned. He had a soft heart. He was, after all, his father's son.

"Does this kid stink?" Mary Catherine asked. She was more like her Aunt Mary Pearle.

Going outside, I looked for the person who was in charge to see if it would be all right to invite the boy. The boss man shouted loudly up to the rooftop. The nasty nose-picker replied. He was the child's adult cousin. He immediately gave his enthusiastic, "I reckon."

Our children charged out of the kitchen door, ready to go.

"Where's the kid, Mom?" asked Butlar.

The boy was relieving himself on an outdoor bench. As he zipped his fly, he challenged, "Over here, but what's it to you, asswipe?"

The two boys bristled. Mary Catherine looked at me and rolled her eyes.

Somehow — it's a blur — I got everyone loaded into the station wagon and headed out to the children's favorite playground-restaurant. I repeated to myself, "This will be fine, it's a kind thing to do. This will be fine; it's a kind thing to do. This will be fine, it's a kind thing to do." All the while, I kept my eyes fixed on the rearview mirror and focused firmly on our guest. Like a mother lion, I knew instinctively, to fear for my own.

My second mistake was in going to an establishment with a playground. We ordered our breakfast and sat down at a picnic table to eat. The meal lasted maybe four minutes. On an up note, the boy's table manners made the Newberry offspring appear almost Victorian in demeanor.

I gathered the trash and mopped up the spilled orange juice.

"You're messy," Butlar told our guest.

"Eat my dust, butthead," replied the urchin.

"Don't even think about it," I warned Butlar, who looked at the boy with lethal intent. "Go play."

The two boys leapt over tables and chairs en route to the play area. "Last one there's a fart face," said a young male voice sounding oddly like my darling son.

Another mother glared at me. I blanched. "Sorry, we're just real excited."

Mary Catherine rolled her eyes and followed the boys at a discreet distance. Sitting back down, I sipped my coffee. *Okay, I can see them. Besides, what can happen? It's a fenced-in area with safe equipment and several of us adults are watching.*

For the moment, the boys seemed to be playing together in a civilized manner. Mary Catherine was swinging quietly. The coffee was pretty good for fast food.

Not twenty seconds passed. *"Maamaa,"* shouted an unfamiliar voice.

I, along with all the other grownups, made

a mad dash toward the sounds of distress. I found Butlar pulling *our guest* off of a pleading child.

"Good for you, Butlar," I said with sincere gratitude and pride. I took the arm of the roofer's child and commanded him to apologize to his hysterical victim.

"Hell no, ma'am," he snarled.

In a voice that came from the deep dark depths of my anger, I gritted my teeth and strengthened my hold on his arm. "Oh, yes, little boy, yes, you will."

His red hair on end, he steadied his feet. "I ain't gonna."

"You are, too, gonna." I held him in a death grip in front of the sniffling child.

"Ain't."

Mary Catherine tugged on my sweatshirt. "Mom, our kid spit on that little boy."

"Any clue why?"

"Our kid said 'the jerk is talking weird.' "

"Weird?"

"I think he could be talking French or something."

Our guest snorted. "Yeah, it was foreign talk, all right!" The boy tried to break free of my grasp. "Let me at him! He's a weirdo!"

I pointed to our car. Emphasizing each word and all but spitting out my teeth, I commanded, "*Go!* All three of you, get in the *car!* And do it now!"

They obeyed.

I couldn't drive home fast enough. Not a single word was spoken. Once there, my two children scattered to far reaches of our neighborhood, where they remained for the duration of the day's roofing job. I watched as the small sociopath bragged about "taking care of the foreign dude" to his grown cousin, the skinny man, who puffed up proudly.

There must have been something harmful in the family's water supply.

Later that night, Mary Catherine slyly asked if any more roofer kids were coming to play the next day.

"No, absolutely not!" Then I prayed I was right.

Sure enough, the roofers returned the next morning, short one boy. He must have had an appointment with his parole officer.

Two days — that's two *long* days later — the job was completed. The crew took cash, cash only, and left in a hurry. Most of them were sprawled in the bed of the truck. All of them whooped and hollered as they screeched off down the driveway headed for where, only the Lord knows. Empty beer cans tumbled from the back of the truck.

Three houses later, we could hear new cans popping open as the pack roared out of our subdivision.

Delighted to be done with the Roofers from *Deliverance,* I vowed to avoid doing any further business with that particular company. I always keep records in my special office drawer about any workmen or companies we have used. Lest I could possibly forget those people, on my list of references, next to their name, in bright red magic marker, I drew a skull and crossbones.

To my horror, there is a *P.S.* to the story. It came last month, when our roof had to be completely replaced, not just the shingles, but the whole blasted roof, right down to the house's original studs.

In other words, this was going to be a big mess, which would cost lots of money. I didn't know the technical names for all that had to be done, but it was crystal clear that a $1,300 gutter job — which was to be completed in one day's work — quickly morphed into a $13,000 gutter-and-roof job with a still-escalating estimate. Along with that, the one-day plan was scratched with a completion date yet to be determined. We were looking at a month-or-longer project.

I inquired as to what might have caused

the expensive problem. The roof man explained, "Well, Mrs. Newberry, I hate to tell you this, but whoever put on that last roof did a really bad job. You folks have probably had some leaking ever since." With that, he walked the entire perimeter of our home poking a long stick at any given overhang I pointed out. Black rot belched to the ground, forming little piles of proof for his diagnosis.

I immediately began to plan a trip to the beach. Beau would be most adept at handling *this* construction job.

At least he wouldn't have to deal with junior roofers from hell.

EVERYONE IN THE CEMETERY ISN'T DEAD

BY HONEY NEWBERRY

Not always, but on occasion, the crazy things that happen to us at home pursue us beyond the city limits. Most dramatically, this phenomenon occurred during a trip to Memphis where we planned, that's *planned,* to attend a family wedding.

Pleased that Beau and I had kept well to our schedule, we decided there was ample time for us to visit my family's gravesite in Memphis's historic Calvary Cemetery. Going to a cemetery may not be a festive idea for some people, granted, but for me it was something I felt compelled to do. My husband humored me.

It was 3:30 on Saturday afternoon. In just three-and-one-half hours, we would be sitting happily with my parents in St. Ann's Catholic Church, enjoying our cousin Kathleen's wedding to Jonathan. We'd looked forward to the event for months.

We had flown in to town the day before.

Just barely. I'd managed to leave our tickets at the baggage check-in desk. The desk was located on the sidewalk outside Hartsfield International Airport, some thirty minutes of walking and train-riding away from where we stood, trembling and, as it were, short two tickets.

Our flight was preparing to board as the authority figure, the airline's crack representative, steadfastly refused to let us check in simply because we were without the tickets. It needs to be said that the woman had confirmed the fact that the tickets had been recovered and were in the hands of the airline's staff. We were told that a "runner" was en route. I prayed he was a man with Olympian speed.

"Rules are rules, ma'am," she kept repeating over and over again. We'd heard her the first time. *And,* this was well before September 11, 2001, and the strict regulations that followed. The woman's smug smile became more resolute with every minute that ticked by.

"Those tickets will probably not get here," she sneered in Beau's face.

"Please, just let us board."

"Take a seat in the waiting area, sir," she ordered as she gripped the microphone. She announced, "Attention please, ladies and gentlemen. We will begin boarding in one minute."

"Look, ma'am, you *know* we have tickets!"

"Siiirrrr, do make some attempt to calm yourself."

Nose to nose, Beau glared at the woman but masterfully managed to restrain himself from cramming the microphone down her throat.

My blood pressure was skyrocketing because I knew full well that my family, specifically my parents, was eagerly waiting for us to arrive. Just when it was apparent that we would be flying on the only other flight, some six hours later, a young man raced up, huffing and puffing. He couldn't speak, but handed us our tickets.

We took our seats mere seconds before the plane took off. In flight, I gave my peanuts to Beau. I couldn't swallow. He couldn't either, but crunching those nuts soothed his disposition. He washed them down with a good, cold beer which also served to temper his state of mind.

To clarify things just a bit, we did have a pleasant Friday, post flight. We'd enjoyed visiting with family, had a wonderful time at the rehearsal dinner party, and the weather was perfection. It was the kind of weather the city fathers pray for when they set a date for the official celebrations of the autumn season. The temperature was warm, with a cooling breeze. The leaves, which barely clung to their home trees, presented a Crayola box full of brilliant hues. The air was crisp and fresh. A sapphire sky was dotted randomly with puffs of cotton white. In fact, at the rehearsal dinner the night before, several people remarked that Kathleen's late grandmother, Ann, had surely ordered the picture-perfect weekend for her beloved granddaughter's special day.

Certainly with Ann in mind — as well as my grandparents and a dozen other relatives — Beau and I began to make our way toward the family plot. The grounds of Calvary cover acres and acres, and finding one's way can be most confounding with the cemetery's twists and narrow, turning roads. So to be absolutely certain we were headed in the right direction, we stopped the security guard and asked him to confirm my foggy directions. He was all too glad to help.

"Yes, in fact, I do remember your people," he assured us. "I knew your grandfather, the old gentleman, a fine man he was. I used to wait on him at the Summit Club." He pointed in a general direction. As he wandered off, the guard again commented to himself, "One fine man, a fine, fine man. Yes, siree."

As I reflected on my childhood visits to my grandparent's home in Memphis, Beau scoured the monument-covered landscape for "my people." In the great forest of angels, tombs, Madonnas, crosses and crucifixes along with every conceivable shape and size of marble marker, Beau finally spotted the site we sought. I placed flowers on the graves and took a few precious moments speaking with those resting beneath my feet. There is a closeness I feel when in the presence of a loved one's burial spot.

All too quickly the serenity of the scene was shattered when my thankfully always time-conscious husband announced, "It's getting late, Honey. Say good-bye, or we'll have to hurry."

Reluctantly, I rose, and we walked to the car. He faster than me.

We again rode past all the familiar family names. The sun streaked across the rolling green landscape. Its shadows seemed to knit the stone monuments one to another. I sighed quietly as I drank in the peacefulness of the setting.

"Crap!" barked Beau as he stomped the brake pedal of our rental car.

"What in the world?"

Not only was Calvary Cemetery's heavy black iron entry gate closed, but also it was tightly secured with a big, heavy chain and a padlock!

I jumped out and hurried to take my turn yanking on the gate. I grasped at a straw and suggested optimistically, "Maybe the nice guard left us a key so we could leave when we were ready?"

"Yeah, right! You're dreaming if you believe that."

I suggested we go to the business office. Of course, no one was there, but we had something of a triumph. "See, Beau!" I said. "Here's an emergency number. You memorize the first three numbers, and I'll memorize the last four. Now, where's your cell phone?"

"At the hotel, on the top of the TV."

"No comment."

"Look, I didn't plan to make a bunch of phone calls from the graveyard."

"Okay, let's move to Plan B. I noticed that there's a house near the back of the grounds."

His dwindling lack of power took control of Beau. He screeched off and drove through the memorials as if he were competing in the Daytona 500. I buckled my seat belt and closed my eyes. "It's a good thing all the residents of Calvary are already dead."

My husband floored the accelerator.

"See, there it is, Beau! The house, right over there!"

He frantically honked the car horn. I jumped out, and like a monkey clinging to his wire cage, I shook the chain length fence. "Help, help, can someone please help us?" I wanted to be heard over Beau's honking. An elderly lady slowly opened her screen door and cautiously shuffled over toward me. "Yeah, whatcha want?"

I explained our dilemma. Beau stopped me before I got to the part about the wedding. "Uh, Honey, we're in a bit of a time situation here."

Over and over, I repeated the emergency number to the woman. Moving at the speed of a dying snail, she shuffled back inside. It took more than ten minutes, seemed hours longer, but she eventually returned to the fence. "I managed to git somebody. They's comin'."

"Oh, thank you, thank you," I gushed.

"Don't get your hopes up," Beau countered.

"And *you* don't be so pessimistic."

We drove back to the entrance. Minutes ticked by as we sat waiting for the rescuer who would set us free. The sun was setting. We wouldn't have any time to relax before the wedding. Even my optimistic spirit was beginning to dwindle.

"I'm going for help," Beau announced. "You stay here, and *if* the guy comes with a key, drive out and pick me up. I'm gonna go to that auto parts store we passed and call a cab."

"Please be careful," I warned.

The last thing he said was, "Lock the car doors."

The cemetery was located in a terrible part of town, one known for weekly, if not daily, shootings, along with crack houses and creepy people in general. It was getting dark. I comforted myself, saying, "At least, you can see Beau every step of the way. As long as he's in sight, he's safe." At that exact moment, he disappeared behind a big, brick wall.

Swallowing, I began to pray. *You're letting your imagination get the best of you,* Creola whispered.

The sun went down. The flaming heavenly body dropped like a gigantic orange bowling ball. Along with the sun went my courage. Shrouded in pitch black, only the car's dashboard gave off any light. I was locked in Calvary Cemetery on Elvis Presley Boulevard. It was the thirteenth day of the month, and every horror movie I'd ever watched began to replay in my head. Beau had been gone for at least fifteen minutes. More prayers. I turned on the car radio.

Ah hah, *Prairie Home Companion* would be on shortly. Surely Garrison Keillor would provide a bright spot. The entertainer/storyteller's radio show had been our delight on many an evening.

"Beau will be back any minute, and we'll have a big laugh," I said aloud, talking to Creola.

Garrison's voice caught my attention. "Good evening, ladies and gentlemen. We're fortunate to have with us a world-famous performer and his ever-popular polka musicale." Polka music. I listened for thirty seconds and turned off the radio. With sincere apologies to enthusiasts, the jubilant melodies from a group of merry-making accordion players made my jitters worse.

SQWEEEEK. "What on earth?" My heart either stopped completely or was pounding so fast I couldn't detect its beat. Sitting in the dark, surrounded by tombstones, my memory summoned every urban legion I'd ever heard.

SQWEEEEK. The dead man's hook! The Lover's Lane fiend! Ready for the kill, his hook was embedded on the rear door handle of a couple's car. The two drove away just in the nick of time. The locked gate . . . I couldn't escape!

SQWEEEK! The radio's aerial retracted into the trunk. Oh.

Forty-five minutes had passed. "Beau, where are you?" I called out the window. "Are you all right?"

I decided to meditate. My friend, Martha, once suggested a phrase. Let's see, oh yes. *The thorn has roses.* I began to chant, "The thorn has roses. The thorn has roses."

I maneuvered into a yoga position despite the car's bucket seats. Sitting cross-legged with my shoes off and the palms of my hands turned up, I closed my eyes, took a deep, cleansing breath and kept chanting, "The thorn has roses, the thorn has roses, the thorn has roses."

It worked. In less than thirty seconds, I snickered. Tension melted.

I turned the radio back on. 6:10 p.m. The wedding was less than an hour away. Where *was* Beau? *He's been knocked in the head, is passed out in a pool of blood, and his wife is doing nothing but laughing hysterically.*

Polka music gone for a moment, Garrison

113

Keillor's uniquely smooth voice gave me a sense of hope. *Thank you, Garrison. I owe you.*

Suddenly, I noticed a shadowy figure coming toward the car. I strained my eyes to see who or what it could be. It was getting closer! In its hand was a large object. An axe? Dear God, who *is* this and what is he carrying? Visions of dismemberment flashed before me. Closer and closer it came. I held my breath believing that somehow, if I tried hard enough, I could make myself invisible. I squinted my eyes and wrung my hands.

The shadow waved. "Honey!"

Beau!

Air escaped my body. I leapt from the car and ran toward him.

"You're okay!"

"Not really," he panted. He was clutching a pair of bolt cutters.

"The security company is — *pant, pant, cough* — is in Kansas City. Can you believe that? Kansas City!" *Deep breath.* "The jerk who answered the phone thought I was kidding. Kidding! That incompetent loser!"

"What'd you say to him?"

"I said, 'Look, fella, my wife and I are locked in a cemetery on Elvis Presley Boulevard in Memphis.' The son-of-a-bitch thought I was joking." *Exhale.* "He asked me if I were with the security company. I said, 'If I were with the damn company, you lunatic, I'd have a key!' He left me on hold for twenty minutes — *cough, cough* — while he called his supervisor. Twenty minutes! Then they *both* hung up!"

I listened in stunned silence. Beau went on, "There's more. *Yellow Cab* refuses to come to this neighborhood. The dispatcher says it's too dangerous." Beau gripped the bolt cutters and proclaimed, "This cutter is the only chance we have. I bought it at an auto parts store."

"O-O-O-Okay then."

He attacked the locked gate. "Turn on the headlights so I can see."

I cranked the car. Lights and polka music. I mashed the radio's *off* button. "The thorn has roses," I muttered.

"I may have it," sputtered Beau. "It's about to give!"

I stepped from the car just in time to hear the *crack.* "Hooray! We're free!"

"No, the bolt cutters broke." He slammed-dunked the tool into a trashcan a good fifteen feet to his right.

"Nice shot, Beau."

"We'll have to walk to the auto parts place," he said.

"How about the motel next door?"

"I went there, first. A prostitute proposi-tioned me."

"Are you sure?"

"The woman said, 'Wanna party?' I told her, 'Thanks, no. My wife is waiting for me. She's locked in the cemetery.' "

"Now, that's funny."

"The prostitute laughed, too."

Before we left for the auto supply store, Beau decided to move the car to a safer place. Wise man. He didn't want to tempt someone to come in and strip the car for tires, parts, whatever. He parked by the cemetery's business office, right under the sign listing the *emergency* number. He growled at it.

We climbed over the cemetery wall. There we stood, looking into five lanes of speeding cars, motorcycles, eighteen-wheel trucks, ambulances, police cars, and cars that looked as if they were returning from a demolition derby. Beau grabbed my hand. "Come on, Honey, run for it."

I just wanted to stay alive long enough to go to the wedding. As soon as we got across, I calmed down a tiny bit. Beau whirled around and said, "Hurry! Run back to the other side. Toward the motel!"

"*What?* First, you didn't even want me to walk by the prostitute, now you want me to run *toward* her?"

"See those guys? I think one of them has a gun!"

"Gun!"

With cars and trucks honking and motorists yelling obscenities, we raced for sanctuary past the lady of the evening. Luckily, she had stepped inside. At the auto parts store, Beau was greeted cheerfully by his new-found friends, including the store's security guard and the clerk who had sold him the bolt cutters.

"So, this is your wife," grinned the guard. I smiled back. I couldn't help but notice he had a severe case of pink eye. I nodded, but could not extend my hand.

The clerk asked if the cutters worked.

Beau frowned. "Not so well."

I uttered not a word. I almost gagged as I watched the guard's eyes ooze.

Apparently, Saturday nights are busy ones for the auto parts business, because there were quite a few other customers. Determined to get to the wedding, I overcame my trepidation and approached a clerk to share our tale of woe. "Is there any cab company that serves this area?"

"Lady," responded the clerk, "you folks might try *Metro Cab.* They may be willing to come out this way." He dialed the number, chatted with someone for a minute, then nodded at us. "You're in luck. Metro said yes!"

Beau raced outside to watch for the cab.

I stood inside, profusely thanking the caring clerk. He scratched his head and said, "Ma'am, you know something? A guy got shot down the street, oh, maybe forty-five minutes ago. Your husband ain't real safe standing out there like that. He could get shot, too."

I ran to the door. "Beau, get back inside! Run! The clerk says you may as well have a bull's-eye on your back!"

"Holy crap!" Beau's eyes were saucer-sized as he strode toward the store. A hefty woman with orange hair and two-inch long purple fingernails came after him. Her gold tooth glistened in the neon lights of the store's sign as she flashed a broad smile. The woman restrained my stunned husband by digging her nails into his shoulder. I clutched my throat and watched as the two of them held an animated conversation.

What would happen next? Within seconds, he stepped back inside, shaking his head and laughing. "Guess what?"

"Another offer?"

"Nope, at least, not an offer to party. The gal said, 'I heard your wife say you two was going to a wedding so I figured you might want to do some shopping. I could give you a *biiiggg* discount on a *veeerry* expensive clock. It just so happens that I have one in the trunk of my car, a real *Seth Thomas.* I *suppose* I could let you have it for, uhhh, say, twenty bucks?' "

"And your answer was?"

"I thanked her and said my wife had already sent a gift."

Up drove *Metro Cab.* Halleluiah! We had maybe twenty-five minutes to get to the wedding. The cab driver not only managed to get us to the hotel but also agreed to wait and drive us to the church.

When we got there, we sat down next to my very anxious family. Mother was holding Daddy's hand, trying to calm him. He'd been looking around the church for us for thirty minutes. She leaned over, patted her chest, and said, "We understood that you were coming early? Did something happen?"

"Nothing much, Mother, just a little car trouble. It's fixed. You and Daddy look wonderful."

"You look nice, too, Harriette. But a bit frazzled, I'd say."

There was no question, my mother knew something was up. "Car trouble? How could you have car trouble with a rental car?"

"Must have been a lemon," frowned Daddy. "Beau should have had me rent one for you."

"Good idea, Daddy. We'll take you up on that, next time."

Beau rolled his eyes.

A hand tapped me on the shoulder. "So what really happened?" whispered Mary Pearle.

With my back to our parents I quietly replied, "Guess where we've been for the last three hours?"

"I give up."

"Locked in Calvary Cemetery."

"Did you say *locked in* Calvary?"

"*Shhhhhh!* I'll tell you about it at the reception."

The music started. The wedding was wonderful.

At eight the next morning, we returned to the cemetery in another *Metro Cab* to retrieve the car. We spotted the very same security guard from the afternoon before.

Beau turned to me. "One car in and one car out. How simple is that? Oh well, let's get the car."

The old guard never as much as looked up.

As we drove past the auto parts store, Beau said, "I should've bought that clock."

CHAPTER 7

When I called Beau from Florida, I reminded him of the nerve-wracking trip to Memphis. As with many other events in our marriage, we could now joke about it. Beau mentioned the post 9-11 security guidelines, saying he couldn't imagine what would have happened to us if those regulations had been in place when we arrived at the gate without our tickets. "Don't you know," he laughed, "that hostile ticket agent must be in her full glory, these days?"

"For sure! By the way, how's the roof job coming?"

"Let's just say I'm not anywhere near laughing about this mess, just yet."

I was even more delighted that I was out of town. I could almost hear the hammering.

After I told him goodnight, I walked out onto the condo's balcony. The peaceful wash of the evening tide welcomed me.

"Poor Beau," I said to Creola.

I could almost see her smile.

The next morning I went for my walk. Now that I'd actually met Beatrice, I was enthusiastic about seeing her each day. I was also intrigued by some of the other familiar faces along my way. We humans tend to stick to our schedules even when we're away on vacation, so I'd often come across some of the same folks. I figure this was either inborn or habitual from years of schooling, jobs, carpools, and all the other time commitments that tie humankind to ticking clocks.

There had been a good number of women walking solo that week. Like me, they wore hats, were gleaming with sunscreen, and more often than not, sported cover-ups. I wondered if their cover-ups were to keep the sun off or, like mine, were donned so the wearer didn't have to hold in a protruding tummy.

Of course, there was always that one muscular, leather-skinned gal. Every beach has one. A show-off in my opinion, the bikini-clad woman ran like a cheetah at the water's edge. She never, but *never,* wore a hat. A sun-worshiper for certain, she avoided all shade to the point of trying to dodge clouds. I imagined the athletic woman to be a former champion water-skier, maybe a Weeki Wachee Mermaid, or perhaps an aerobics instructor. Most likely, Leather Lady worked as a stripper.

Couples with small children came and went from week to week. I would see a family for just a few days, but to my regret, those vacationers tended to disappear by the next weekend. I always enjoyed seeing the children and yearned for the days when Beau and I, Mary Catherine and Butlar built our own sandcastles.

I also kept an eye out for honeymooners. I would offer an encouraging smile, but rightfully so, the two would be far too wrapped up in one another to notice my greetings.

The one thing I enjoyed seeing was the occasional dog. I specifically liked coming across the big black ones. Black dogs with red collars would always tug at my heartstrings. I would look into the eyes of any black canine who came my way, and remember my own beloved Nestle.

Leave it to me to name a dog after chocolate.

I hurried back to the condo to work on that story.

MISSING NESTLE

BY HONEY NEWBERRY

It was a June night in 1995. Beau and I had enjoyed a quiet dinner out before Butlar's high school graduation hoopla began. When we returned home, we expected Nestle to gallop through the kitchen and greet us at the back door with her traditional, tail-wagging frenzy. This night, however, the dog was nowhere in sight.

Beau and I called for her. No pup.

We walked around the block shouting her name. No response.

We got in the car and drove around searching, whistling, and shouting, "Nestle, Nestle. Here, girl." Nothing.

Nestle could always be found in one of three places — on the deck, on the family room rug, or wherever in the house I happened to be.

I phoned the neighbors. No one had seen her.

Although Beau attempted to reassure me,

and I him, we both became more and more frantic as minutes ticked by. Nestle had never been more than two or three houses away, and that was always with one of the family members in sight. It was getting very late, dark as pitch, and our dog was still missing.

Butlar came in happily talking about a neighbor's graduation party. "We had so much food! Everyone was there. It was awesome!"

He called for Nestle. He suddenly noticed my tear-stained face. "What's wrong, Mom?"

"Oh, Butlar!"

Beau told him that our dog was gone. Reacting exactly like we did, our son bolted from the house to look for her. Like his parents hours before, Butlar searched first on foot, then from his car. Our son had loved Nestle since the sixth grade, when he had picked her from a litter born next door in the neighbor family's tool shed.

No one in the Newberry home got a minute's sleep that night. Just after the sun came up, Butlar was sitting at the kitchen table pushing scrambled eggs around his plate. Unable to eat a single bite, he dissolved into tears, "Mom, I don't care about my stupid graduation. All I want is Nestle."

We were shocked. Since the Christmas holidays, he'd counted down the days until he graduated. He'd thought of little else.

Had someone stolen her? Not a chance. Had she run away? Never, not unless something had really frightened her. Nestle was terrified of fireworks. Had there been some that night? The answer was yes. Fireworks were shot off at the neighbor's graduation party. Butlar blamed himself.

For two days our search continued. By that time, Mary Catherine arrived home from college and joined in the search efforts. We contacted the humane society, the pound, and our veterinarian. The doctor's staff alerted other vet's offices all throughout the area. We put up signs with Nestle's picture and name and our phone numbers. Night after night, we searched. Night after night, we grew more and more discouraged. The temperature climbed well into the nineties. On the front walk, our family's yellow cat, Tasmania, stood sentry for his lifelong companion. In his opinion, the big dog was his mother.

Day three, in desperation, I phoned a lady I hardly knew.

"Mary, Mary Hannah?"

"Yes."

"I'm not sure you'll remember me, I'm

Honey Newberry. Our daughter Mary Catherine went to school with your twins."

"Um, hmm."

"A couple of months ago, you kindly stopped your car to ask if my dog needed help. We were over by the country club entrance sitting under your neighbor's tree. We must have looked pretty pitiful!"

The woman hesitated, "I think maybe I remember."

"I explained it was terribly hot and that Nestle and I were just resting. You mentioned that our dog reminded you of your two Labs."

"Yes, I definitely do!"

"Well, this time, I'm afraid we actually do need your help. Nestle does. She's lost. We figured out that she was frightened by our neighbor's fireworks a couple of nights ago. I'm hoping she'd wandered over your way."

It was a stab in the dark. Mary's neighborhood was a car ride of some seven miles from our home.

The kind lady tried to encourage me and promised to keep her eye out for our dog. Even so, two days had passed and the temperature was hovering near one hundred degrees. Water? Food? Would our dog's intimidating size keep people from trying to get near her? Probably.

Day four, I returned home to find a message on the answer machine. "This is Mary. I may have spotted Nestle! Call me right away!"

Shaking, I could hardly push the telephone's buttons. Mary answered, "Yes, I think it was, at least, I hope it was your Nestle. This big black dog was wearing a red collar."

I grabbed my purse and crashed headlong into Beau and Butlar. "Back in the cars! Someone's spotted Nestle!"

"Mom, I'm going with you," said Butlar, jumping in my car. Mary Catherine hopped into the front seat of Beau's.

We wound through the quiet neighborhood, around a golf course, street after street. We stopped, quizzing anyone we saw. Fifty-five minutes later, there was still no sign of our dear dog. No one had seen her. At the traffic light onto the four lane, traffic-filled Peachtree Road, I turned to Beau. "Think she tried to cross?"

"Maybe, Mom. Go for it!"

I anxiously scanned the busy street fearing I would see Nestle's furry black form laying dead in the gutter. No body. Whew. Relieved, I gunned the gas pedal and wheeled left into heavy traffic. Unexplainably, I believed we were going in the right direction.

On the other side of the street, two ladies were taking a walk. I screeched to a halt and all 6'2" of Butlar jumped out of the car.

Gesturing wildly, he likely terrified the women as he shouted, "Excuse me, have you seen a big black dog with red collar?"

"Yes, we have!" The taller of the two turned to point. "We did see a dog like that down that way. You might know the area. It's near those new condos on Roxboro Road. You'd better hurry though, the dog we saw seemed disoriented and extremely weak."

"Thank you!"

We wheeled away. Tears of hope flooded my face. Butlar shouted, "Yahoooo!"

One traffic light held us, then another. "Change light, change!" we chanted.

Green! We were free!

Taking a deep breath, I tried to plan how we'd react upon finding our traumatized pet.

"Butlar, that women said the dog they saw was disoriented. We must try to act calm. If not, we'll spook poor Nestle. We certainly don't want her to bolt and run away from us."

"I understand, Mom. But do you really

believe we'll find her?"

"Yes, I do. I've believed that from the first night." Just as I had done for the past four days, I was trying hard to convince myself as well as to convince my son. "Butlar, call your Daddy's car phone and tell them where we are. I just have a hunch."

"Yes ma'am!"

"Drat! Another light."

Suddenly, Butlar screamed, "Mom! Look over there. It's her!"

Our dazed dog stumbled out from behind a long bank of cypress trees. In her bewildered state, sweet Nestle was staggering farther and farther east and away from our home.

Butlar and I leapt out of the car and ran toward her. Waving our arms, we shrieked her name, "NESTLE! NESTLE, GIRL, come! Nestle, Nestle!" Both of us were hysterical with relief. So much for our strategy of the cool, calm, and slow approach!

Nestle stopped. She tucked her tail. Butlar and I grabbed our precious bedraggled animal and tackled her to the ground. About that time, Beau and Mary Catherine drove up. They rushed over and collapsed into our jubilant reunion. We five rolled around on the median as Nestle panted and

131

licked her very relieved family. People in their cars stared at us. Some honked and others applauded.

Nestle was alive!

We helped her into the car. Butlar honked my horn in celebration all the way home. He hadn't been that excited since the Atlanta Braves won the pennant. The exhausted dog lay shaking quietly on the back seat. She was confused and oh-so-weak. Her paws were raw and bloody; the pitiful pup was terribly dehydrated. Once safely in our kitchen, Nestle collapsed on the cool tile floor. I propped her chin on her water dish and she drank two bowlfuls without a pause.

Beau drove to the yogurt shop. He returned with a quart of Nestle's favorite flavor, golden vanilla. He sat on the floor beside the dog and fed her yogurt spoon by spoon. Her parched but eager tongue licked clean every bite.

Nestle was home.

Butlar begged to take the dog to his graduation, insisting that the ceremony was to be held outside in a football stadium. "Who would care?"

I agreed with our son, but Beau thought better of our idea. Butlar's grandparents, Aunt Mary Pearle, his cousins, his sister, Beau and me, and an enthusiastic contingent of friends would be audience enough for the occasion. But Beau was adamant. "Nestle will be just as happy to attend Butlar's party, afterwards."

"With lots of yogurt!" said Butlar.

"*And* no fireworks!" I added.

CHAPTER 8

I sighed at the sweet memory of Nestle's homecoming as I waded out into the water and splashed my face. My eyes filled with tears. Just that past May, Nestle had to be put to sleep. A good old girl, she would have turned fourteen the following October.

Nestle no longer greeted every visitor at our kitchen door, nor did she nap on the deck or on the rug in the family room. No longer did she wrestle with Butlar when he dropped by, nor did she follow me to every room in our house. Our beloved pet was buried in the far corner of Beau's garden. Her favorite toy, a hot dog that squeaks, marks the spot.

A white miniature poodle scampered down the beach toward me.

"Hey, puppy," I said, and waved at the owner. I petted the dog. He licked me in return. His tongue seemed so tiny in comparison to Nestle's. I wondered if the poodle liked yogurt. Nearby, a feisty red dachshund frolicked with a beach ball twice his size. I called out, "That little puppy has no idea she can't get the ball in her mouth."

"That doesn't keep her from trying," grinned the old gentleman who accompanied her. "Would you like to pet her? Her name is Hildebrand Von something or other. My wife knows the whole high falutin' deal. I just call her Hildy."

I jumped at the chance. The dachshund rolled over on its back and let me rub her stomach. "So soft! You're such a cutie, Hildy!"

"Madame, you've made a friend for life."

When Mary Pearle and I were growing up, we had a little dachshund, a female, the only girl dog we ever had. Shortly after Creola took us to see the movie, "Peter Pan," Mother surprised us with the puppy. The film fresh in my mind, I insisted we name the dog "Tinkerbell."

Tinkerbell loved to eat and we took great pleasure in feeding her. The poor dog got so fat that Daddy changed her name to "Cowbell." Eventually, the name "Bellie" stuck. It suited her well.

Beau knew well my love of red dachshunds. When Nestle died he offered to replace her with a puppy just like Bellie. I declined. It was dear and sweet of him, but for me, there'd never be another dog.

"Bye, bye, Hildy."

I walked on. An older couple was headed my way. They never failed to greet me, he with his hearty, "Good morning, young lady," and she with her sweet smiles. The two also never failed to be dressed in matching shirts. They were always holding hands. Not once had I seen them unmatched or unattached. I assumed the couple held hands not for safety's sake, but because it came naturally.

More than once, I almost stopped them so we could talk. I wanted to get to know them. I yearned to hear their story, their stories, to learn the secrets of such tender love and obvious devotion. I never followed through with my plan because it seemed intrusive.

Rather, I delighted in making up fairytales of the couple's life together; about how they had worked hard but happily toward their mutually determined dreams, and now, how they looked forward to every break of dawn.

I knew they must surely appreciate music of every kind, along with literature, the classics for certain, and poetry, too. He likely tinkered with tools, woodworking perhaps? She, or better, the two of them, painted pictures of the shore. It was a given that they kept a garden.

I fantasized that they had moved around the country, finally settling into a charming retirement cottage by the Gulf of Mexico, one overflowing with music, art, photographs, books, and fresh flowers.

Creola whispered to me. *Honey, you lazy girl, always making up stories are you! You should be writing.*

As if on cue, Beatrice strode up behind me. "Well, hello there!"

I halted, startled. "And how are you today?"

"I'm just fine, as fine as a fiddle, particularly because my darling Jennings is set to arrive anytime now. But, you Harriette, how are you?"

"How could I be anything but happy on such a beautiful morning?"

Beatrice looked at her watch. "Agreed! It is a gorgeous day, my new young friend, and I can see that I have exactly the perfect amount of time for a walk with you. What do you say we take a pleasant chat-walk?"

"Chat-walk? Oh, I see. Sorta like a cat walk but with words?"

"A clever play on words, dear. Off we go!"

We strolled up the beach. "So Beatrice, what are your plans for your son's visit?"

"Well, I'll just have to wait and see what he wants of me. Usually the poor boy is so exhausted when he arrives that he simply collapses on the porch in order to rebuild his energy and his creativity. Jennings is a starving artist, you see. Actually, he's not starving. He works as an accountant in corporate America by day. Mercifully, he feeds his soul by night with his writing. I eagerly await someone's discovery of him, a great talent is my Jennings."

I didn't hear the last part; I was hung up with *that* word. "Writing."

Beatrice stopped, picked up a shell, and said, "Now, dear, take a look at this shell. Here's a curious mystery for us to ponder. Don't you just have to wonder what kind of interesting creature lives inside this lovely house?" She put the shell to her eye. "Anybody home?"

I didn't have the heart to tell her the shell was empty, that a seagull had probably eaten the inhabitant. This wise old beachcomber was idealistic in so many ways, ways that endeared her to me.

Beatrice sighed at my smiling silence. "Sometimes I speculate that my house is but a shell, too. And one of these days a giant will come along and pick it up to peek inside. Most assuredly, that fellow will amuse himself with the lifestyle of a certain Beatrice!"

"Will the giant find you at home?"

"But, of course; I couldn't bear to miss such an event!"

"Beatrice, I'm very curious about your shell. I doubt you are among us ordinary condo dwellers."

"No, I'm not, but I do know how *divine* those condos are. Actually, they hadn't begun to build condominiums when I started coming here. I came by ship with Ponce de Leon!"

"You must have discovered the Fountain of Youth."

"Harriette, you are a honey."

"Okay, now I know you must be a psychic! My friends call me 'Honey.' My real name is Honey Newberry. I don't know why I didn't tell you that in the first place. Harriette is my given name."

"Bully then, *Honey* it is. I must add that you look more like a Honey than you do a Harriette. A Harriette would have to be stiff and superior, and most definitely, if you will excuse me, she might even be rather homely."

"You've described perfectly my Aunt Harriette, the woman for whom I was named!"

"Oh dear me, I do apologize," said a suddenly red-faced Beatrice. "I AM so sorry!"

"No offense taken."

"My dear, I *meant* that I am sorry for your aunt, that poor, dear woman!"

The two of us giggled like teenagers.

"So, please, Beatrice, if you will, please tell me more about your home. I'm a house person myself and relish finding out about my friends' habitats. One's home says so much about a person's spirit. My curiosity is a bizarre and rather rude habit, but I can't help myself."

"It's not rude at all. I'm pleased that you're interested. Mine is a cottage, one built around the turn of the century. That's the LAST century, you understand! We bought it in the 1960's or 70's; I don't really recall other than to admit I've come to this area for decades. My home is a mumble-jumble of mismatched furniture, the artwork of friends, books, and treasures from my travels. So crammed with precious memories is it that were the house a boat, it would surely sink."

"Sounds fascinating to me. One of these days, I may surprise you and pop by." The moment the words left my mouth, I regretted my brazenness. It was not at all like me to invite myself somewhere.

Beatrice put her hands on hips. "Jolly well,

140

how about joining me for a glass of fresh-squeezed orange juice on Monday morning? We can enjoy the juice and visit after our break-of-dawn constitutional."

Back-peddling, I stammered, "Gracious, I've never been quite so forward. Please excuse me!"

"Forward? Sounds to me more like you're being honest and interested. Honey, I like a lady with spunk. We're set for Monday, then?"

"I suppose so."

"Besides, I'll need company after Jennings departs. His exit always leaves me feeling rather glum."

We walked quietly for a minute. Suddenly she said, "I see a gorgeous diamond on your left hand. Should I assume there is a Mr. Newberry?"

"Oh yes, his name is Beau; Honey and Beau. Think we could be from the South? I think 'Honey and Beau' sound as if we fell out of a magnolia tree in the sprawling front lawn of a white-columned home."

"Charming. Why, in my opinion, Honey and Beau is a perfect pairing of names."

"Let's talk about you, Beatrice. Do you have a Mr. Beatrice at home?"

The woman threw back her head, and laughing wildly, replied, "We'd be here through the winter were I to start on my matrimonial sagas." She slapped me on the shoulder. "So tell me, do you and your darling Beau have any little honey bees in your hive?"

"We have two children, Mary Catherine and Butlar. They are marvelous, of course. Aren't all children?" Now, Beatrice, you keep changing the subject. "You've mentioned Jennings. Did you stop after achieving such a level of perfection in your son?"

"You're correct. Jennings is my crown jewel. But don't dodge my questions. I'll not relent now. I already know about me and mine; I simply must learn more about your and yours. Tell me, dear, where do you and Beau, little Mary Catherine and Butlar live?"

"Atlanta."

"My son's city!"

"Hmmm. I have an idea. After I go back to Atlanta, you might encourage Jennings to accept an invitation to our home for dinner one night?"

Beatrice replied only with a vague shake of her head. "My boy is just so preoccupied. Besides, you know these young people — rarely do they follow their mothers' suggestions. Honey, you are a darling to even consider going to such trouble. So thank you, but likely no."

I sensed some tension and decided to change the subject. "I should clarify something here. My children are all grown up. Mary Catherine works for an advertising agency in Chicago and Butlar is in graduate school at the University of Georgia."

"Remarkable! So, dear heart, tell me about this empty nest of yours."

"It's a long, long story. I'll go into that at another time, but suffice to say, we bought a suburban fixer-upper in nineteen eighty-two and have been working on it for more decades than I care to admit!"

"How lovely."

"And you? Where do you live, Beatrice, when you're not at the beach?"

Beatrice launched into a monologue. I discovered that she was, indeed, a very well-traveled woman. Calling herself "something of a vagabond," Beatrice was much happier answering "where" questions over family topics. My friend's list of domiciles began with "whenever I travel in Europe," or "when we lived in Hong Kong," or — the most extraordinary reply of all — "when my husband, now let me see, which one was it? Oh yes, of course, Godfrey, when Godfrey worked for Her Majesty in London —"

"*Her Majesty,* as in Queen Elizabeth?"

"Oh my, that was so long ago. No dear, my Godfrey worked briefly for the Queen Mum."

I smiled. Could it be that this Beatrice actually knew Ponce de Leon?

Beatrice checked her wrist watch. "My dear girl, it's getting on in the morning. You and I have walked for so long that I'm starting to show my age! I hope you will have a happy and a most productive weekend."

Productive, there she goes again. Pushing me to work. Sounding like Creola.

"Thank you, Beatrice, but, lest you forget, I am on vacation. This gal won't be doing anything productive!"

"Whatever you say, dear. I will look for you on the beach Monday, just as the sun comes up. Don't forget, Honey Newberry, and you are to come by for juice afterwards. Ta Ta."

"I'll be there."

My whimsical friend strutted away. I stood and watched until she disappeared beyond a distant sand dune. I could hardly wait until Monday. I wanted to see the amazing Beatrice's home.

You ought to spend the weekend writing, Creola whispered.

I ignored her.

■ ■ ■ ■

Without Beau around, the weekend crept by. Saturday's rain only made things worse. As soon as there was a break in the weather, I grabbed my purse. Checking to make certain I was armed with a couple of credit cards, I got on my bike and peddled across a bridge to a beachside village.

In and out of antique stores I drifted. Even though the spending demon was calling to me, not one purchase did I make. This, for Mrs. Newberry, was a first, particularly as I was on vacation. Beau would be proud of me.

I concluded that shopping solo was a very boring activity. Proper browsing required at least one girlfriend and two or more was preferable. Even shopping with Beau was better than by myself. I actually missed my husband's habit of fidgeting like a child. He didn't mind spending money so much as he minded his wife's showing him every potential purchase.

"Get whatever you want," he would desperately announce from his seated position. Commonly known as the "husband chair," this most comfortable seat is always conveniently located in specific sections of the nicer shops. "My feet hurt," he'd complain. "Are you ready to leave yet?"

"I'm sorry, dear. We'll go right away. Just let me pay for this one thing." I would motion for the salesperson and cheerfully take home the very item I'd spotted an hour before.

Riding my bike back across to the island, I passed a young family of four. I ached for our now-grown children. Mary Catherine hardly had the time to call, much less visit. Butlar's graduate schoolwork was all-consuming. He had even less time to come. A proud mother was I, yet seeing the young family at play made me wish for what was over.

I pulled into a video rental store and got a movie I knew Beau would despise. Popcorn and a movie, this would be an apt solution for my blues. Robert Redford.

"Perfect," I said aloud.

I rallied.

CHAPTER 9

Robert Redford notwithstanding, I was delighted when the weekend finally came to an end. On Monday, I woke up early. My excitement to see Beatrice's place roused me from bed like a bugle call. I slid into my slippers, threw on my robe, and turned on the kettle.

Stepping onto the deck, I took a sip from a mug of hot tea. The sky was not yet tinged with pink. Checking the clock — I surely didn't want to be late — I gobbled a breakfast bar and poured my regimen of vitamins onto the glass table.

One of these days, my family would find the lifeless body of Honey Newberry. The story in the newspaper will read: "The Georgia author apparently choked to death on a calcium tablet."

Unscrewing the cap on a bottle of water, I picked up the calcium and a multi-vitamin whose label read "for seniors." I raised my eyebrow at the idea of being regarded a "senior citizen." Heck, I remember well being a senior, a senior in college. Time certainly had a wicked sense of humor. Had I changed? Hardly at all, I concluded on this day that held so much promise.

With another swallow of water, I took my controversial hormone along with an aspirin to avoid a heart attack. Next I took my allergy medicine, a mystery pill the health food store clerk assured me would grow fingernails, something for my eyes, and vitamin E to stave off brain loss. My mother's frequent lament rang in my ears, "Growing old is not for sissies."

With the tablets successfully consumed — I hadn't choked to death — I took off my nightgown and began to squeeze into my bathing suit. The Robert Redford film, hmmm, popcorn had swelled my fingers enough that my rings couldn't make it over my knuckles. *Salt.* The suit presented a greater challenge than usual.

I reached for my cover-up. Sunscreen, hat, I was good to go. I hurried from the condo onto the beach. Like clockwork, I came across the handholding couple and pictured myself with Beau. That he would soon be at the beach for the three-day weekend pleased me.

The eastern horizon, painted with pink streaks, slowly made way for the glowing orange ball. Becoming more vivid with each splash of the surf, the sky opened and gave birth to the sun. The sight never ceased to overpower me. For a moment, I was totally spellbound by the grandeur of sunrise.

I saw Leather Lady pumping and prancing down the beach. Some fifty yards behind her sprinted a man who could have been the woman's masculine double. A marriage made in heaven! Had I not been in a hurry to meet Beatrice, I may have tried my hand at matchmaking.

A small, brunette boy and his father worked side by side on a sandcastle, one nearly as tall as the child. The boy was happily building turrets with his red bucket, while his dad, who worked with the intensity of a building engineer, was scooping out canals in a frantic effort to stem the rising tide.

A baby girl cried from her seat beneath a large umbrella. Her concerned mother fretted about the rising sun's changing angles and adjusted the infant's pink terrycloth hat to shield her face.

As a group of laughing women passed by, I began to worry that something could have happened to Beatrice. I was concerned that

Jennings's visit had proven too much for her and that she wasn't quite up to the morning's activity. On the other hand, I was also hopeful that Jennings had decided to stay an extra day. How nice to imagine that Beatrice was still relishing his company.

On I walked.

"Come at once!"

Alarmed, I quickly turned around. I didn't see anyone, but it was Beatrice's voice.

"What's wrong? Where are you?"

"Hurry!"

I followed her anxious voice behind a sand dune. I found Beatrice standing there happily, almost breathless. She pointed to a mound of sand topped with small yellow flags. "Turtle eggs!"

I had seen many such mounds all along the beach. I'd observed the turtle-patrol people, but never before had I witnessed such an intense show of enthusiasm. From what I had already learned about Beatrice and her diverse interests, it was fitting that she be one who would take up the plight of the baby turtle.

As I attempted to listen attentively, Beatrice, the turtle woman, provided with me more information about sea turtles and about their threatened offspring than I would ever need.

150

"You must come with me when they hatch. It is quite a happening!"

"I'll be there."

Beatrice cupped her hand to demonstrate. "A newly hatched baby is no bigger than a silver dollar."

"My goodness."

"Yet they grow up to become huge sea creatures."

"Amazing."

"Yes, those precious few who make it, that is. You simply have to be there to believe it. Hundreds of wee ones come forth from the sand and scamper toward the water. I swear to you, it is more exciting than human birth!"

Beatrice's arms and legs began to flail about. She dropped down on all fours. The elderly but intensely energetic lady began to crawl quickly toward the surf, looking more like a crab — a somewhat *clumsy* crab.

Concealing my laughter, I cheered her on. "Go, little turtle, you can do it!"

She had a good fifteen yards to travel. I danced along beside her, yelling, "Go, go, turtle, go!"

Seconds later, much faster than any turtle could have accomplished the same feat, Beatrice victoriously paddled into the Gulf. She swam out a good twenty yards. Springing up out of the water, she shouted, "I made it, I made it, I'm going to be a big turtle some day!"

A man jogged toward me. "Is that woman crazy? Does she need help?"

"No, no. She's just victorious."

"Different strokes for different folks." He tipped his baseball hat and continued on his way, though he turned around so he could run backwards for a few yards, staring at Beatrice warily.

I threw my head back and roared.

"Who was that?" asked Beatrice, wading out of the tide.

"Just some runner; he offered to rescue you! Guess he didn't realize you turtles must claim the sea."

"Some humans have no sense."

"Guess not."

"This turtle is all worn out. Come on. Let's go have our juice."

Laughing, I linked my arm in hers.

Beatrice's beach house was everything and more than I expected. Like its owner, the house was ageless. Surrounded by porches, the inside of the structure was awash with light. Every wall was painted white and floor to ceiling was covered with paintings and tapestries. The blond hardwood floors were enhanced with handwoven rugs, orientals, and painted oilcloth.

Pottery and sculptures adorned every bookshelf and tabletop with some of the larger pieces arranged dramatically in groupings on the floor. Books were stacked everywhere and frequently topped with curious pieces of art. Several gorgeous silk fabrics hung from the ceilings giving the rooms a dreamlike feel. Each piece of Beatrice's furniture seemed to be at home. All were interesting, some were antique, some art deco, while others simply defined comfort and invited a guest to sink into soft, welcoming cushions.

I felt as if I were standing in a magical space. "Beatrice, your cottage is truly wonderful. I'm drawn first to one amazing object and on to the next. I've never seen anything to compare."

"My dear, thank you, but the truth is that I have far too much here. One of these days, I'm sure to disappear into all my clutter." She chuckled as she handed me a tall glass of freshly-squeezed orange juice.

I could neither credit my thirst to the walk and Beatrice's uproarious turtle imitation nor to the elation of seeing my new friend's home, but, for whatever reason, the juice was the most satisfying beverage I'd tasted in months.

Beatrice threw open the porch door. She spread out her arms and invited in the warm Gulf breeze. "Good morning, world!"

We sat gazing through the porch's screen and silently watched as peaceful waves softened the sand. I thought about the little brunette boy's sandcastle and wondered if it were holding its own against the tide. Little matter, it's the building of the castle that matters.

What was it about salt air that made me breathe so deeply? Why was I suddenly starting to feel emancipated?

"Beatrice, tell me please, what do you most appreciate about your home?"

For the first time, the older woman began to invite me into a tiny part of her world.

"You are sitting squarely in the middle of much I revere. My greatest loves surround me in this cottage. I am thrice-blessed. First, I have all that is within these walls. Secondly, I have incredible beauty readily observed from the ease of my chair. Thirdly, I have the immeasurable pleasure of sharing these gifts with the people who come, visitors like you."

I quietly nodded my head, thanking her.

"Aren't we comfortable in these soft, cushy delights, dear girl? Every woman needs to bask in an overstuffed chair. Don't you agree?"

"Definitely. I've died and gone to heaven."

"One doesn't need to die to experience paradise."

"Agreed." I drank in Beatrice's words with the same pleasure as I'd consumed the orange juice.

Beatrice took note. "So to answer your question, I have the sea and the sand; and as you can see, I also have my art, music, literature, and the cottage itself. These are my passions because they come together to remind me of my friends, my Dear Ones. What you see in my home needs to be shared with others, with *you* at this moment, my Honey of a friend. As of this day, you are invited here any time you wish. Borrow my books, my music, and my art should you be able to carry it off. It's to be enjoyed."

"You're too kind."

"No, I'm not, I require that my friends dust anything they borrow. You, too, would be required to follow my rule."

I laughed.

"You think I'm kidding, do you? I'm forever trying to make a dent in all this disarray!"

I laughed again.

Beatrice suddenly jumped up. "What am I thinking? Music, we must have music! What do you like?"

I perused a wall of CD's and tapes along with too many records to count, including 45's and 78's. Overwhelmed by the choices, I urged my hostess to make the selection. Pleased, Beatrice placed a Mozart CD in the player.

"One thing I now want to hear, Madame Newberry, is you talking about *you*. Tit for tat, I've answered your query." She winked at me and ordered, "Now you must answer mine."

I shifted in my seat.

"But first . . . I nearly forgot!" With that, Beatrice abruptly hurried into the kitchen. I assumed she was going to get more juice. When the lady returned, however, she had a very familiar item in hand. Much to my surprise, Beatrice was holding one of my books.

"You are such a humble little thing, Mrs. Newberry. Most of my author friends go on and on talking about their work. Getting you to mention yours was like pulling hen's teeth!"

"So how did you know who I am?"

"I knew about you before you even moved in. You see, ours is a small and closely knit community. A friend of mine was browsing in the village bookstore one day when the excited owner announced that a rather well-known Georgia writer had just stopped by. The owner, Sonny Gilmore, was all aflutter. When you left, he announced to everyone that the author was asking about a place to rent."

First as a child, then with Beau and our children, I'd always vacationed at the opposite end of the beach. Only my last-minute decision to come necessitated my finding this particular place. Our favorite rentals had long since been reserved. In venturing farther south, I not only found the bookseller which led me to Miss Eugenia's condo, but also and most fortuitously, I met Beatrice.

"I've rented beach condos in the vicinity before, but —"

"Sonny's the one who put you in touch with Miss Eugenia, the pleasant woman who runs the ice cream shop two doors down from him. I believe it's Eugenia's condo you are renting?"

"Yes, it is."

"Anything Sonny Gilmore knows, everyone knows. Telling him something is like alerting Paul Revere."

"So, Mr. Gilmore said I was *well-known,*

157

did he? I must drop by and thank him. I could use the publicity. Are you sure those were his words? 'Well-known?' "

"Don't be getting too puffed up, dear. It doesn't take much to enliven the inhabitants of our little hamlet."

I grabbed my chest and making a piercing sound as if I'd been stabbed. "So it doesn't take much, does it? Why don't you plunge a knife straight through me?"

"Oh my dear, this time, it is I who must apologize. I certainly didn't intend to deflate you. Truthfully, the first time we talked, I made a mental note that you were one young woman who could use some creative encouragement."

"Obvious, was it?"

"Do you remember the day I turned the cartwheel? Well, that was this old girl's blatant attempt to meet the famous, yes, that's *the famous* Georgia author."

"I'll be darned."

"Now, Mrs. Newberry, will you *please* sign your book for me?"

"Of course, I'd be honored."

She presented the book to me along with a gold pen. I wrote:

"To Beatrice, may this be the beginning of a meaningful and joy-filled friendship, one which started with a cartwheel! I hope you will enjoy this little yarn half as much as I am enjoying my visit with you on this glorious June morning.

Fondly, Honey Newberry"

"Lovely," Beatrice said.

I looked into the wise woman's eyes. "I must tell you the truth, Beatrice. I've not been writing lately." I confessed to her as fervently as if I were confiding in a priest.

She smiled. "That's something I hoped you would discuss with me. It can be most freeing to bare one's soul to a stranger."

I eyed her in disbelief. "You're hardly a stranger to me, Beatrice. Tell me, what gave you the idea I was struggling?"

"Ah hah, the fine art of deduction. When I went to the bookstore and saw a display of your novels, I noticed that it had been more than three years since your last work was released. Your reluctance to tell me your real name when first we conversed convinced me that something was amiss. I'd like to suggest that your lack of output may benefit from a strong shot of Beatrice *joie de vivre!*"

It was as if the woman were reading my mind.

Creola Moon, you had a roll in this, didn't you?

"You're off in dreamland, Honey Newberry. Tell me, my author friend, what seems to be your problem?"

"Nothing specific. It's as if I'm out of gas."

"Ah hah! You've done the right thing by coming to the shore. I know, because I'm blessed with the friendship of *many* creative people. It's as simple as this. Your vessel is empty, yes. However, time by the sea — and away from your typewriter — will surely serve to refill that vessel."

"Sounds as if you've been there, too, eh, Beatrice?"

"Dear girl, I've been *everywhere* at one time or another. It comes from living a very long life. Gracious, did I say 'typewriter'? Now *that's* proof positive I'm as old as the sand!"

"Typewriter, hmmm. That's an idea. Beatrice, do you think I should trade in my computer for an old-fashioned typewriter? One author-friend of mine absolutely refuses to abandon his trusty Underwood. The man insists that computers are nothing but a curse, and feels that all publishers should ignore anything written on one. He also says that no decent writer with any pride in his work would be caught using such an *easy* method!"

"Poppycock. Your friend is simply too set in his ways. Methinks it could be that the proud fellow is fearful that he's not technically adept enough to learn how to use the computer."

"Could be."

Taking my last swallow of juice, I said, "I appreciate your encouragement, but I don't want to spend all our time discussing me. Let's just say that, for the present, I'm a professional beachcomber!"

"Whatever you decide, dear."

Something about her glance, not unlike Creola's familiar knowing look, told me she and I weren't finished with the topic.

"Now, Beatrice, would you mind if I took a quick tour around your home?"

"Of course not, but may I suppose we are merely going to take a short break from the subject at hand, err, the subject of beachcombing?"

"We'll have to wait and see."

"I can be a formidable force, Madame."

"And I can be a hard nut to crack!"

"Let's call it a draw for now, Mrs. Newberry. Please feel free to acquaint yourself with everything and at your own rate of speed."

"I'd be happier were you to grant me the

pleasure of a *guided* tour."

"Gladly, I've rested long enough."

"Are you sure you're all right, Beatrice?"

"I'm always all right, dear girl. Besides, walking amongst my treasures invigorates me."

Beatrice and I strolled about the living room. My friend handed me a beautifully hewn wooden mask. "A young artisan in Africa presented this treasure to me, oh, some fifty years ago. Isn't it stunning?"

"Quite stunning." I gently moved my fingers over the intricate features.

Beatrice selected a bowl from a grouping near a window. "This bowl was made by a gifted Native American potter from Santa Fe. One can almost sense her euphoria in the creation of such a marvelous piece. I'd think you might share a similar feeling as you fruitfully script a novel?"

I made no reply. She smiled wickedly.

An hour later, Beatrice and I were still touring the living room. Each painting, each sculpture told a story, a story of the artist and a story of Beatrice's acquisition of the piece. I found myself to be as intrigued with the stories as I was awed by the beauty of the art. Beatrice's face took on the most soulful expressions as she shared tales about her exceptional collection. The woman was a storyteller. Several times, she wept as she looked upon her possessions.

To my surprise, I wept along with her.

My spirit was coming to life in the art-filled cottage. I'd always flourished on emotional expression. Being in Beatrice's home was like drinking from a cool mountain spring. Even as a young child, I would weep at the splendor of a finely done painting or from the sounds of beautifully performed music. I was once labeled "cry baby" by an insensitive classmate when I shed tears upon hearing the words of a stage actor's perfect rendering of a line. I paid no attention to the silly boy. I was too engrossed in the play to be bothered. Nothing lifts me higher than the triumph of another's soul reaching her artistic best.

It was as if Beatrice's art collection were passing that power on to me. Beatrice was the conductor of a great, artistic, symphony orchestra, while I was seated as first violin.

Beatrice studied me gently. "I gather you are enjoying the tour?"

"I have no words to adequately express what I'm feeling." I wiped a tear from my cheek. I closed my eyes, exhaled, and cleared my throat. "Some of this work, Beatrice, is *yours,* isn't it?"

"Perhaps. A couple of my pen and ink

drawings are stuck around here somewhere. There's nothing spectacular to show you, however. Here, do take a look at this painting. Can you not taste the tartness of the crisp green apple?"

"A Granny Smith, no doubt!"

"Possibly."

"Please confess, Beatrice. Tell me which works are yours."

Beatrice would take no credit for anything. She only emphasized that the sculptures, the paintings, and the weavings were exceptional acquisitions from her "Dear Ones."

"Jennings?" I pried.

"My son's talent lies more in his prose and poetry. Sadly, one of the difficulties that holds back the boy is his humble reluctance to share his remarkable gifts with others."

Like me, you mean. I thought it but didn't say so.

For a few minutes more, Beatrice showed off one piece then another. Often, the artist's name was kept secret by her determined placement of a thumb or her reluctance to turn over the sculpture. The work itself became the focus of our conversation; its beauty, its line, and its form captivated her concentration. Yet Beatrice would passionately talk about the sometime nameless artist's life, about his struggle, and, most emphatically about his triumph.

"Writing must bring its own challenges?" she asked.

"They call it 'work' for very good reasons," I replied.

"Please assure me that the agony of your exercise is eradicated by an appreciative readership?"

"Most certainly. For me, one generous compliment can cushion hours of editing angst! Beatrice, are you being honest when you insist that you are not a writer? You are too well aware of creative trials to be a novice."

"As I mentioned before, I'm merely a student of human nature, that's all. Oh, perhaps I may have written a poem here and there, but nothing to match your charming novels."

I smiled. "I don't believe a word you say."

I paused to admire a pen-and-ink sketch of an unusually handsome older man. On the bottom right, I was certain I saw the name "Beatrice." On a second sketch I saw the letter "B," and on several others, "Bea." Again and again, a version of my friend's name appeared. As if it were an unspoken rule, I intuitively knew not to push Beatrice for an explanation.

I clearly understood that I should take the

woman just as she was with no questions asked and without coercing her to share her secrets. I'd simply appreciate Beatrice for the person she was willing to be. Anything that she wanted to reveal, I would cherish.

The mood was suddenly broken when Beatrice made a pronouncement. "This has been a lovely visit, but I realize you have other things to accomplish, as also is the case with me."

I glanced at a clock. "Oh my goodness, I've stayed far longer than I intended! Thank you, Beatrice, thank you very much. I cannot tell you what this day has meant."

"My joy, dear."

We walked toward the door.

"Oh, one last thing, if I may. Tell me about Jennings's visit."

The enchantment washed from her face, Beatrice sighed. "Dreadful. In fact, he didn't come at all." She stood erect, and with a shake of her head, she gathered herself saying, "Jennings knows well that his mother understands. And forgives."

"I'm so sorry."

Beatrice threw back her head. "And what, pray tell, do *you* have to be sorry about now? Young lady, have you ever taken a count of all the 'sorry's' you say in a given day?"

"No, ma'am. Maybe I should."

"Well, it could do you some good. In truth, I relish my son's absence, for it gives me extra time to anticipate his next appearance."

"Yes, of c-course," I stammered. "I should go now."

Beatrice nodded.

I waved sheepishly, turned, and walked slowly down the beach. I deeply regretted the negative end to an otherwise perfect morning. Not only had I overstayed my welcome, but I'd also brought up a painful subject which destroyed the day's magical mood. I hurled a broken shell as far as I could. It landed with a splash. "Honey, you should have had enough sense to realize Beatrice would have told you *if* she wanted you to know."

We all have our sad secrets, Creola whispered.

The phone was ringing as I entered the condo.

"Beatrice, here!"

My spirits lifted at the sound of my friend's upbeat tone. "Hello! I'm so sorry we . . . that is, I'm not 'sorry,' but —"

"Young woman, just so you understand.

I'll expect a short story from you by week's end."

I didn't bat an eye at her demand. "Consider it done!"

I put the phone down and gaped at thin air.

I could hear Creola chuckling.

CHAPTER 10

I turned on the computer. The logo came up. *Ball and chain.* Beatrice's challenge weighed heavily. No! Wait a cotton-pickin' minute, actually Beatrice's challenge weighed *lightly.* This day, *lightly* was the more fitting adverb for my rejuvenated outlook.

Had the morning provided such an intense aesthetic experience that the fog finally lifted? *Creola, what do you think?* Had I just been depressed all this time, as Beau suggested? Who knew? Not me. I could only compare my improved mood to watching the mist on a mountain lake as it gives way to brilliant sunshine.

The screen saver came into focus. A close-up shot of Nestle's face greeted me. I could almost hear our dog's tail beating against the study's floor. For nearly fourteen years that faithful dog had curled up next to me as I wrote.

I had to give credit to Beatrice for her

encouragement and for sharing her magnificent art collection with me. *And Creola, I have you to thank, too. As always, your spirit plays a role in all that I do.*

I looked at the screen saver once again.

"Nestle, I *am* getting back to work."

The first thing I pulled up were a few random notes I'd made a long time back concerning Creola. Her face focused clearly in my mind's eye. I could almost feel her touch, hear the whisperings of her voice. Creola's laughter would fill a room as her energy flourished seemingly without limit. Yet there was something in her carriage that spoke of pain and suffering, courage, faith, and strength. Those were the traits I later learned to appreciate.

When I was a child she was the ideal playmate, one with endless stories, a source of games and ideas of things to do, but also a source of strength, who cared for and cherished our whole family. As I grew up and met challenges in own life, Creola became a fountain of wisdom for me.

Music had always played an important role in our family's life. I could remember many nights when Mary Pearle and I were young and we spent evenings together listening to dance bands on the radio. As they often did, our parents would get up and whirl in one another's arms around the living room. Naturally, we joined in as the four of us spun about in circles!

"Dear, just take a look at your daughters," beamed Daddy. "With your good example, these two girls will soon outshine their old man!"

A picture of myself, Mary Pearle, and Creola came before me. Many an afternoon after school, the three of us would roll back the living room rug, turn on the record player with a stack of 45's, and dance around to the music of every recording artist from Elvis to the stars of Motown. By the time Mary Pearle and I enrolled in dance class, we could have taught every step.

How such a chubby lady as Creola could move around so gracefully, I would never understand! Clapping and lifting her feet, turning and strutting, Creola taught us everything she knew about dancing. All the time, she encouraged us to make Mother and Daddy believe that they were our skilled instructors.

I stretched my arms and leaned back in my chair. *Creola, you had to have been well into your forties in those dancing days.* I could almost hear her chuckling. Now I was so much older than she had been when I judged her to be downright decrepit!

Yes, she was definitely laughing.

What a difference the visit with Beatrice had made. Thinking about my age didn't depress me nearly as much as it had only one day before. I was beginning to appreciate the wisdom that comes with passage of time. *Thank you, Creola. You're accomplishing your mission. You, too, Beatrice.*

I cannot count the number of discussions Mary Pearle and I had concerning our nanny. As little children, we only knew that Creola shared every day with us. She simply appeared from the bus stop and, other than telling us funny stories about her parents, never mentioned anything about herself. We were adults before we even saw where she lived.

Our childish theories of her origin ran the gamut from a runaway nun to a former striptease dancer, and from an earthbound angel to an actress who, bored with stardom, escaped from Hollywood to live in Humphrey.

Mary Pearle once suggested that Creola's surname of Moon was made-up.

"Moon is all about magic spells. It's obvious to me, little sister!"

I disagreed. I believed that Creola's last name had a heavenly connotation. "Mary Pearle, you're wrong about spells. I know that the moon is filled with angels, angels just like Crellie. For some reason, she wanted to leave the moon, so she hitched a ride on a falling star."

"Sure, and landed right here in Humphrey?"

"Yes, to be here with me."

"With *us*."

"Okay, with us."

I was beginning to suspect that the same kind of mystery surrounded Beatrice, a lady who didn't even admit to having a last name! More likely, she simply avoided the subject.

Comparing the two, Creola and Beatrice shared traits beyond their secretive backgrounds. Each has made an impact on me. Each rarely thought about herself, but was concerned about the well-being of others. Each woman had a great zest for life and an enormous love for those around them. Importantly for me, however, was that both women had a knack for bringing out what was and is the best in me.

Now *here* was a theme.

I began to type.

THE VISIT

BY HONEY NEWBERRY

To me, Creola was always Creola. She wasn't black, she wasn't white; she was simply *herself.* Throughout the turbulent years of integration, I tiptoed around any mention of the racial turmoil whenever Creola was present. Creola kept to the same undeclared decree. A decade would pass before I addressed the subject of prejudice face to face with her.

Weary of the invisible but impenetrable wall between us, I finally decided to approach Creola. After I was grown, I called her at home and drove the fifty-mile distance that separated us. Over and over, I practiced what I was going to say. I rethought, worried, and almost changed my mind about broaching the issue at all. Rehearse as I did, I still couldn't come up with exactly what to say. I just knew I was determined to say *something.* On I drove.

As I had done so many times, often with

Beau and our children alongside me, I pulled into Creola's front yard. The dust of Georgia clay covered my car like a crimson cloud. As it settled, I could see Creola waiting on the porch of her weathered but tidy clapboard house. Geraniums in clay pots lined the steps, and two large lacy ferns hung from the rafters. Creola had likely been out there for an hour or more, anxious, and unquestionably praying for my safe travel. She rose to her feet and grinning, came to the top of the steps holding wide her still strong arms.

"It's sooo wonderful to see my Moonbeam!"

As the two of us sat sipping sweet tea, we discussed the things of our lives. We talked of family, of shared memories, of illness, of day-to-day events. We also talked about the weather, a favorite subject of hers. She'd always loved summer storms, relished the excitement!

Creola's weather radio, a gift years ago from Mother and Daddy, broadcast reports around the clock. I could hear it playing from inside. Never much of a television watcher, Creola readily admitted that she enjoyed her weather reports. "Technology, *pfffttt*. Why 'technology' is just another word for the devil," she insisted with a spit. "But

I do appreciate the Butlars' fine, fine weather gadget. I like to know what the heavens have coming next."

"Oh Creola, there's just nobody else like you."

" 'Course not, child. The good Lord makes us all different."

I nodded. We sat quietly for a moment. I looked around her yard. "I see you have firewood still left from the last year."

"Ready for the next. Hope it won't get too cold, though. The last ice storm kept me inside for way too long. Couldn't get to church."

I studied her old pecan tree and two sweet gums. Her flower beds were bursting with buds. "Looks like your daylilies are close to blooming."

"Ummm hum."

I was just making small talk. Creola sensed it. "Why have you come to me on this day? Anything wrong?"

"Nothing's wrong, but you know me, Creola. I do have something on my mind."

"Best get it said, then."

"You and I are so close. I can talk to you about everything in the world, everything short one subject."

Creola's cautious eyes peered into mine.

"You're not having troubles with Beau, are you?"

"No, heaven's no!"

"Thank the good Lord for that. For years I've grieved myself brittle-boned over Mary Pearle's unhappy choice. One of these days, she'll see that man for the scoundrel he is. I was almost hoping that was why you came today, to tell me he was dead!"

"Creola Moon, I can't believe you said that."

"I'm telling the truth like it is."

"Crellie, please don't get me started on Edgar today. You and I always egg one another on. We're gonna have to stop talking so viciously about that man."

"Like I said before, it's simply so."

"You've always seen him clearly, while I continued to wear rose-colored glasses much of the time. Guess the 'little sister' in me recalled their wedding, their romance, how handsome Edgar seemed in my eyes back then. Why, I even used to believe that Edgar's daughters might manage to soften their father. I hoped that having a family would make Mary Pearle and Edgar happy."

"Doesn't work that way, sorry to say. I was like you, though. I always wished the darlin' babies would improve him. But a man like Edgar isn't about to change. Not in his nature." She shook her head. "I just praise the Lord that my Priceless Pearlie's girls have all of their mother's goodness and not one ounce of their father's badness."

"I agree."

I sipped iced tea then twisted a little gold ring I wore on one pinkie. Showing it to her, I said, "See, it fits perfectly now. Remember when I was eleven and you gave it to me to replace the ring I lost? I keep it with me always."

"Of course, I remember. Don't recall ever seeing a child so upset about losing anything. I'd have given you my head to dry those tears! It fills me with joy to see you wear the ring."

"I wear it often, Creola, especially when I'm talking in front of an audience or reading to a group of people. Anytime I'm nervous about something. It remains my good luck talisman."

She looked at me harder. "So, my Moonbeam, why do you need good luck sitting on my porch?"

I took a long, deep breath. "Creola, something has been eating at me for years. Most definitely, this is a very difficult subject."

Creola's eyes locked on mine. It was as if she were trying to help draw out my clumsy words. "Keep talkin'."

"There's an uneasy barrier between you and me." I closed my eyes. "The racial barrier."

Silence.

"Neither you nor I have ever acknowledged our differences, Crellie, nor have we let them interfere with our love or respect for one another. I hope not, anyway." I cleared my throat and took another sip of tea. I also twisted my ring.

"Crellie, I want to apologize to you if ever, with insensitive words or selfish actions, if ever I've offended you." I gulped the tea. "Darnit, Crellie, I guess I'm trying to apologize for being ignorant. No, it's not that, either. I suppose I'm trying to say I'm sorry for being, ummmm, for being naive. Oh heck, Crellie, I'm apologizing for acting, well, acting so *'white.'*"

I never felt more self-conscious. Or any whiter.

Before I could make a worse mess of my well-intentioned efforts, Creola stopped me. Taking my hand, the dignified woman responded. "There is nothing to forgive, baby girl. We are all God's children, you and Crellie. You are white because God meant for you to be white. For the same reasons, He planned for me to be a person of color."

I listened.

She smiled. "And you and I both know that everyone falls short of His plan in one way or another. Us included. But unhappily for us, Miss Moonbeam, because you and I are also created to be different, we may never completely understand one another. Just believe, more than anyone else on this earth, you will always be tied to me like my very own."

Tears welled up. "Crellie, I couldn't love you more if I were."

"That I have always known. You weren't born of my body, child, you were born of my heart. You must always understand there is no black and there is no white where you and I are concerned. That little ring, the one you are about to twist into shreds, that ring sealed our bond years ago."

I relaxed my fingers and placed my right hand in my left.

Creola rocked back in her seat. "I've pondered about this, well, let's see, this *situation,* too. Try to think about us in this way: We are like two big trees standing side by side."

I nodded toward her yard. "The pecan and the sweet gum?"

"Yes, you're getting it! Our leaves, our

180

roots, our barks are different. As close as we stand to one another, and as much as we care about one another, we will never be the same. Not on this earth, anyway. But, dear girl, we remain in our good soil, again side by side, sheltering one another, and standing tall together. We always will. Now, how about a piece of cake?"

"I'd like that a lot."

We ate most of Creola's apple cinnamon cake. Like us, the cake was a fine mixture of a lot of good and tasty ingredients.

Nothing else needed to be said.

But on my way home that day, I questioned my intentions. Guilt? Asking for forgiveness? At least, Creola and I had removed one stone from the wall. Honesty between two people was a beginning. I would never come to accept or to understand the narrow-minded prejudices of other people. I only knew that my relationship with Creola was one nourished with love, trust, forthrightness, and mutual respect. I hoped those shared qualities would forever keep open my mind.

My fingers flew over the keyboard as a story about Creola came to life. It wasn't birthed on the pages of a typewriter, something I did momentarily consider in honor of tradition. But just as sweetly, CREOLA'S MOONBEAM, printed in large, bold type, filled my computer's screen.

It is particularly gratifying for me to write about people I love. In fact, so enthused was I that I wrote well into the night, sleeping only briefly. The sun was already toasting the sand as I scurried down onto the beach. Not only had I missed the usual passersby, but I was also too late to meet Beatrice.

Honey Newberry, either you don't write a single word or you can't make yourself quit.

That said, I know my patterns well enough to understand that these obsessive traits often produced my best work. Plodding along the shoreline, my mind naturally drifted back to Creola. It suddenly dawned on me that her story could well be turned into a book. For once, Creola didn't comment, but a pelican flew overhead as if to say, "I agree."

I watched a family splashing about on a raft and decided such a book could appeal to both adults and to children. When I used to read to Mary Catherine and Butlar, it was always pleasing any time the story was as intriguing to me as it was for my children.

I picked up a shell and skipped it out across the water. I laughed, excited. As

Daddy used to say when a project suddenly started going well, "We're cookin' with gas, now!"

LITTLE SISTERS AT THE ZOO

BY HONEY NEWBERRY

Creola had promised me and Mary Pearle that, come rain or shine, we were going to the zoo in Atlanta. Sure enough, we awakened to the sound of raindrops on the bedroom window.

"Don't you be fretting, darling girls. Of course, we're sticking to our plans. Your mother says it's all right with her as long as there's no thunder and lightening. But you two have to wear your galoshes *and* keep your raincoats fastened. And we must get home well before dark."

"Yes, ma'am!" we chorused.

"Don't you know, those animals get mighty lonesome on rainy days. Not many children come to visit them when it's wet outside. Yes, my darling girls, I'm almost grateful for this gloomy day because we'll have the zoo park all to ourselves."

Because Creola didn't drive, we would take public transportation for our outings in

Humphrey and for our trips into Atlanta. Much of the fun of going to Atlanta for me was riding on the Greyhound bus. Mary Pearle didn't share my enthusiasm. She thought it strange that Creola made her sit up in front with me while she rode in the bus's very last seat.

"How come you do that, Creola?"

"My dear, it's so you girls can see what's just ahead. I choose to be in the last place so I can see what's behind," instructed Creola. "You never know what might be catching up to us."

Mary Pearle was getting old enough to understand the real reason, but I never questioned the seating arrangement. To me, Creola was the source of how best to plan everything. Mainly I enjoyed riding way up high and considered little else. I liked to look down into the cars stopped at traffic lights. "Makes you feel real big," I pointed out to Mary Pearle. Mary Pearle felt plenty big enough already and much preferred the front seat of an automobile.

As well, my sister got irritated with me for frequently embarrassing her. That day, as a case in point, just on the outskirts of Humphrey, I stuck out my tongue at a little boy in a car stopped beside the bus. The boy just happened to be in Mary Pearle's class in school.

In response, he put his thumb in his ear and made a face at me and at Mary Pearle, too. Mary Pearle was simply appalled by the whole incident. It was bad enough that her younger sister called the classmate's attention to their sitting in the Greyhound, but it was even worse that she'd acted like such a little brat.

Creola came forward, shaking a finger. She spoke to me for starting the disturbance and to Mary Pearle for acting stuck up. "I'll tell you something else," Creola concluded, "that little boy would likely give up his week's allotment of cookies to be coming along with us."

"Yes, ma'am."

Creola returned to the back of the bus.

The rain had become but a gentle mist as we ran to the zoo's ticket window. Each of us pulled Creola by a hand.

"Do slow down, young ladies, or you'll be out of energy before we go inside!"

"The lions first!" squealed Mary Pearle.

"No, the elephant," I argued.

"He smells too bad. Let's go to Monkey Island."

Taking her hands from us, Creola intervened, "Don't you know, girls, the black bears will be the most excited of all this day?"

"Why's that, Crellie?"

"It's as simple as this. Bears just love the damp weather. It reminds them of the days they roamed free in the Smoky Mountains. The mountains are washed with rain nearly every day, and the bears miss that refreshing wetness. They will be frolicking to beat the band on this soggy morning."

"Let's go to see bears!" Off we skipped. Creola followed behind, chuckling and scurrying as fast as her feet would carry her.

Just like Creola said, the black bears ran and rolled around on their backs and climbed up and down their tree. It was a fake tree, one anchored to the stone floor of their pen. Those playful bears didn't seem to mind.

"Why is it that the bears had to be taken away from their mountains, Crellie?" I asked. "Don't they get awful homesick? Aren't they missing their families?"

I always remembered Creola's answer.

"My Moonbeam, I'm sure they do miss the other bears. I'm pleased to hear that you care so much. But you mustn't concern yourself." She put arm around me and said, "Listen to old Creola, now. I believe these bears are willing to sacrifice for you and for all the other children. The good Lord gives them courage so you and your sister and the other visitors can enjoy seeing them and learn about their ways. They've likely gotten accustomed to their new way of life, and you know they get lots of good food to eat, too. Just watch them. Look! Didn't that small one up in the tree just smile at you?"

"I guess so." I wasn't convinced, but I hoped Creola was right about the bears being content.

Mary Pearle took my hand and said, "Harriette, I'll go see the smelly old elephant if you really want."

Creola smiled. "You're a sweet girl, Priceless Pearlie. Priceless, too, is my little Moonbeam. Yes, Lord, there's much about my own way of life that I have grown accustomed to. Maybe I'm just like that grinning bear who climbs the cement tree."

CHAPTER 11

Why I hadn't written about Creola before now was beyond me. The time has a way of making my plans for me. But I could hardly hit the computer's keys as fast as memory dictated. Oh heck, I'll admit it, Creola was ready for me to write, and she was whispering in my ear, cheering me on.

Most heartwarming of all, I was reliving the joyful time of being Creola's Moonbeam.

Happily lost in the 1950's, the phone's ringing was like a slap in my face. I despised being interrupted when I was on a roll. Still, it could have been an emergency involving Beau or one of our children, so I answered.

"Hello," I said flatly.

The voice on the other end greeted me with a cheery, "Good morning, sleepyhead. I missed you this dawn."

Had it been anyone else at the beach, I would have begged off saying I was busy with my new book. The caller, however, was Beatrice.

"I'm truly happy you called. You'll never believe it, but your inspiration was the very tonic I needed. I've begun a story and am two chapters into a full-blown book!"

"I'm not the least bit surprised. I could see the light coming into your eyes yesterday."

"Did you?"

"Of course, I did."

I wondered if my friend could be my guardian angel in disguise, but I immediately dismissed the idea. I realized that the angels I'd known about hadn't been married an undetermined number of times. Besides, my angel's job had already been taken by Creola.

"Now, my productive author-girl, you must ignore my untimely interruption and get back to your passion. My news shall wait. I'll call you in a day or two. No, even better, you call me when the time is right."

"No, ma'am, I shall not! You've got my curiosity going now."

Beatrice hesitated. Then, "I did want you to come by. But I certainly didn't mean to halt your progress, particularly now that you're generously giving me the credit for breaking the evil spell."

"Exactly, Beatrice. That spell would still be holding me hostage had it not been for you. I'll be right there."

After saving the story on the computer, I hopped on my bike.

"Faster than a speeding bullet?" said Beatrice as she opened the door. "Oh, I see, you came by wheel. Do come in."

She offered me a diet drink and reached for something on the mantelpiece. Turning around, Beatrice handed me another one of my books. "Would you autograph this one for me, please?"

I was all too happy to sign the book, but was also somewhat puzzled. "Where did you get this copy of *Spinster's Petticoat*? It's been out of print for years."

"Oscar found it for me."

"Oscar? Who's Oscar?"

"He's an old Scottish fellow, a dear friend of mine."

"A member of the famous group of 'Dear Ones'?" I asked.

"The dearest," Beatrice replied.

I could only speculate what that must have meant. "I see."

"Oh no, you don't see!" Beatrice laughed. "He's a darling man, but his red hair keeps him out of the sun most of the day. As a result, the dear fellow haunts all the local merchants, the book store being his favorite spot. You may recall, I mentioned that a friend was in the shop when you came by looking for summer lodging?"

"Ah, so that was Oscar?"

"Quite so. Sonny and Oscar. Each had a hand in telling me about you. Anyway, following my *faux pas* concerning your Aunt Harriette, I immediately dispatched him to find your Aunt Harriette's story. After my impertinent comment, I felt compelled to read about the somber woman! There's little wonder Auntie Harriette never married."

"You didn't find it funny?"

"Well, I suppose I did snicker a time or two. How about the chapter where the nearsighted fellow came to call on her and mistakenly attempted to escort her bewildered mother out the front door instead!"

"The truth is, the young man would have had a much better time with Grandmother than he had with my aunt. It was such a shame Granddaddy stopped him!"

"Dear, dear, had I but known about maiden Harriette, I could have given her one of my husbands!"

"Really? Which one?"

"Now, Mrs. Newberry, you are in dangerous territory."

I desperately wanted Beatrice to talk about

her marriages but that subject was clearly taboo, beyond her wry references here and there. I smiled at her. "I should go down to the bookstore. I really owe Sonny and Oscar a word of thanks."

"Nice idea, dear," said Beatrice. Her mind seemed elsewhere.

"I need moral support when I visit a bookstore. I have an ongoing nightmare where I come across my books in a front window with a sign on them: 'All books on this table $1.00 . . . or will take any offer for multiple purchases for books written by Honey Newberry.' "

Beatrice laughed loudly. I nudged her arm. "Say, Beatrice, won't you come along? We could have a bite of late lunch. I'll gladly go and get my car, if you'll join me."

"Thank you, but I'm afraid it's too late in the day for me to venture out. Besides, the bookstore is only open Thursday through Sunday, so I'm afraid you'll have to wait, as well."

"Actually, Beatrice, that's good, because I don't want to lose the momentum with my story. I'll go by Sonny's on Saturday."

"Excellent plan."

"Oscar sounds like an amenable fellow. Have you been friends for a long time?"

"That's one question too many, young

lady," she said as a tease, but one framed in authority. "Do you have time to tell me about your new book?"

"I'll take time, Beatrice. After all, this is due in large part to you."

"Don't you dare give me credit, Honey. It's the beach and your own talent that are doing the writing. Go on, what's your topic?"

"All right, Beatrice, *if* you insist, you shall remain credit-free." I mimicked Beatrice's accent as best I could.

"You're a brat!"

"So I am. Anyway, it's entitled *Creola's Moonbeam* and is about the nanny who watched after my sister and me. Creola Moon was a wonderful, magical, loving lady. She named me 'Moonbeam' or 'Miss Moonbeam,' when the notion struck her, and my sister was her 'Priceless Pearlie.' "

"*Creola's Moonbeam.* What an intriguing title," exclaimed Beatrice.

"I like it, too. 'Crellie,' I often called her, was a glorious woman. The story will be about Crellie from my point of view as a child and also looking back at her with an adult's perspective. I will gear the book for children and adults, which broadens its appeal."

"Marvelous idea! I can hardly wait to read

what you've written thus far."

"Now, I'm the one with a resounding 'No' to *you! I never, but never, let my friends read anything until it's finished."

"Oh fiddle." Beatrice feigned disappointment. "Then let me ask you something else. Does this burst of energy mean that you also plan to work on those funny stories you've brought up from time to time? You know how I love to laugh. So will other readers, my dear."

"Heavens no, Beatrice. I pitched the entire manuscript in the trash, kit and caboodle, before I came down here."

"So they're gone?"

"Well, a few of them are still in my computer, but —"

"Deary me! Since you won't allow me to read *Creola's Moonbeam* I automatically assumed you'd let me peruse your other stories. Such a shame."

"I feel terrible. Here you are, my magnificent encourager, and I'm letting you down."

Beatrice actually poked out her lip! I laughed. "Aren't *you* the spoiled girl?"

"On occasion."

I thought quickly. I could print out the cemetery saga. Maybe the roof debacle, and, perhaps, a couple of magazine articles. Hmmmm. "Tell you what, my friend, you have a deal. I'll gather up some of the stories for you. After all, you have become my muse. A writer as vain as myself never turns down a willing reader. Besides, you can always use the stories to start the charcoal for your barbecue."

"Don't be so hard on yourself, Honey dear. Now, go!" She shooed me out the door. "Fetch those stories!"

I laughed and nodded. I wanted to get back to Creola right away. I could feel her spirit calling to me.

A Ring and a Promise

BY HONEY NEWBERRY

It was the summer I was eleven-and-a-half. Mother had taken Mary Pearle to camp and I was left at home with Daddy and, of course, with Creola.

I sat on the steps of the front porch tying tight my tennis shoes. I could hear the ballgame playing on the black-and-white television as Daddy's cigar smoke floated out through the screen window. Daddy was crazed with power. He was never, but never, allowed to smoke in the house. With Mother driving my sister to Tennessee, he thought he could get away with his solitary act of defiance. Little did Daddy realize that Creola had a nose like a bloodhound and would be ready to jerk a knot in his neck the next morning when she came to clean.

Fireflies lit the sky like Christmas Eve as I ran across the street for the nightly game of hide and seek with the neighborhood children. In a world full of kids playing, we thought, no, we *truly believed* that our games were more fun, more competitive, more thrilling than any other children's games, anywhere.

Unlike current times, there was little or no traffic, neighbor's yards were nestled next to one another, and there were no fences to hold us back. Even better, a forest of trees, not so perfect gardens, and numerous garages and dusty sheds made for limitless and welcoming hiding places. The girls, usually Mary Pearle, me, Margaret, Betty Ann, Dannie, Mary, Carol, Jackie, and Pamela Jane teamed up against the boys, Chad, Jerry, Dan, Mike, Eddie, Marvin, Fred, and David.

Over and over again, one of our number counted to ten while the rest of us hurried off to hide. Sticky with sweat, hair stuck to our faces, we screamed and shrieked as we jumped out from our hiding places running hard as we could for *home* . . . many of us secretly yearning to be tagged "it."

"Five, four, three, two, one!" I counted. My eyes squeezed tight, my head pressed to the pecan tree in our across the street neighbor's huge grassy front yard. "Ready or not, here I come!"

All too quickly the graying evening sky, streaked in pink, turned to blue-black darkness. Adult voices invaded our play.

"Harriette! About time you came inside," shouted Daddy.

"Ten more minutes, Daddy, pleeeeaassse!"

"That's what you said ten minutes ago."

"This time I mean it."

"*Ten* minutes."

"Yes, sir."

Ten minutes flew like ten seconds. Soon Pamela Jane's mother was calling to her, then Jackie's, then Chad's and Eddie's. Daddy's whistle would come soon. Sure enough, *Tweeaaattt!* "Harriette Ophelia Butlar!" His voice reached through the heavy moist air like a prison searchlight in pursuit of an escapee.

"Coming."

I plopped down on the kitchen chair and kicked off my tennis shoes. I'd lost the bandage covering my hide-and-seek mishap from a few nights before.

"Need a new Band-Aid?" asked Daddy.

"Nope, look, it's pretty much healed."

"How about some ice cream to cool you down before bedtime?"

"Chocolate?"

"Coming right up. Two scoops?"

"Three? It was real hot out there, Daddy. Three and I won't tell Mother you were smoking cigars inside."

"Three and you won't tell *Creola.*"

"She'll know."

"Maybe I should offer *her* some ice cream?"

I laughed at him. "Won't ever work, Daddy. Crellie will get you good!"

I dug my spoon into the cold chocolate. Suddenly I noticed my right hand. I hurled the spoon onto the table. "My ring! Daddy, my ring's gone!"

"Did it fall off while you were playing? Why don't you take a quick look in your room."

"No, Daddy, I'm sure I had it on at supper."

"Okay, then, we'll go search." He stood up, grabbed two flashlights from the kitchen drawer, and handed one to me.

Our ice creams could turn to mush, I didn't care.

Daddy and I hunted for an hour. We shinned our lights around the pecan tree, on the ground and in the grass, all through Mother's azalea bed, in the bushes, the Harrison's tool shed, and every place I could remember playing that night. Nothing. The ring, my amethyst birthstone ring, the ring I got when I turned ten-years-old, was nowhere to be found.

"I'm so sorry, honey. Maybe it'll turn up."

"Oh, Daddy," I wailed. "I hope so."

I was in my bedroom when Mother called to tell us that she and Mary Pearle were settled into the motel near the camp. I heard Daddy say he'd be glad to see her on Tuesday. They kept talking, and I thought surely he'd tell her about the ring. I felt even worse when it dawned on me that he would call me to the telephone and have me tell her myself. My heart was pounding.

I had been extremely jealous of Mary Pearle's going to the fancy camp in the mountains, especially since I would have to wait until the next year when I was old enough to go with her. Sometimes, I hated being a younger sister. Seemed to me Mary Pearle was always ahead of me in one way or another. She'd held her camp over me all springtime bragging about "my new camp shorts, my new sleeping bag." But, that night, her fancy camp and her new stuff didn't matter. I wasn't mad at my sister, I was just mad at myself.

"Hi, Mother. Okay, I guess. No, ma'am, I'm *not* okay. I didn't come when Daddy called, so I lost my pretty ring."

"I'm sorry, dear. Perhaps you shouldn't have worn it outside."

I didn't want to hear that. I wanted

Mother to say, "You'll find your birthstone next to the garage door near the gardenia bush." Mothers are supposed to say those things. That night my mother didn't help me one bit.

Neither did Daddy. "Harriette, it's getting late and I have to get up early in the morning. Please calm yourself and get into bed. Your ring may turn up yet."

"Hope so."

"After all, it is only a ring."

"Daddy! You just don't understand!" I ran into my room, closed the door, and cried myself to sleep. I dreamed that a nasty green bug carried my beautiful birthstone deep down into his muddy home. Thunder roared and lightening crashed. I sat straight up in my bed. My ring would surely be washed into the Gulf of Mexico.

Creola arrived the next morning. I could hear the coffee perking. She marched into my room. "Aren't you the sleepyhead today, Miss Moonbeam."

"Oh, Crellieeeee, my pretty purple ring is lost! We were playing hide and seek last night and it musta fallen off when I was chasing somebody. Daddy and I looked and looked. Do you think some bird might have gotten it?"

"Let's us just see about this situation."

She pulled me into her soft, caring arms.

Forgetting breakfast dishes and everything else she'd listed for herself to accomplish, Creola took the yard broom and motioned me out the door. I still had on my pajamas, the summer kind, however, that looked like a shorts set. She and I searched the morning through, but like Daddy and me, we had no luck. The bright sun didn't help any more than flashlights had the night before.

We sat on the porch. Creola seemed as despondent as I was while we sipped Kool-Aid over ice from our Dixie cups.

"Now we're not giving up, little girl, just so you know. But you and I are going to have to do a temporary thing here. Bad events always call for positive actions. A type of a good luck charm is what we'll try next." Creola went inside and got a cigar out of Daddy's secret box. She knew exactly where he kept his stash. Unwrapping one, she pitched the cigar in the garbage can and slipped a cigar band around the ring finger on my right hand.

She closed her eyes. "Blest be, Angel of Finding Lost Things, I call upon you to yield my Moonbeam's precious gem. If not, please grace her with something even more special. In the meantime, Angel, bring comfort to this grieving child as you bless this very rare work of paper art. Praise be."

I wondered if that was a voodoo prayer, since Creola came from New Orleans, the home of voodoo. But I didn't say anything. With that, Creola got back to her chores and I went about my day feeling much, much better.

Sadly, the incantation provided peace for only a short time. That night it rained again, making me toss and turn, worry and wish for my real ring. So nervous was I that I picked and peeled at the cigar band until it got lost in my covers. I was too tired to look for it. I eventually dozed off and didn't even hear Daddy leave for work or Creola arrive.

"Good morning, Moonbeam!"

"Now I've lost my *new* ring, Crellie," I moaned sleepily.

"Don't you worry yourself one second. I have another solution for us, my darling child."

I sat up in my bed.

"A long, long time ago, when your Creola was a pretty young girl, I had a boyfriend."

"You did?"

Creola had never before talked about such things. I was absolutely astonished. Part of me wished Mary Pearle was there, while most of me relished her missing the special revelation.

"Most folks called him 'Fish,' even his own people, 'cause he was always going fishing. But I called him Lukus, his given name." Creola signed. "Seems everyone but me forgot his real name."

"Was Lukus handsome?"

"Why, yes, he was tall and lanky; the brown of his eyes were as big as walnuts, and he had the biggest, best grin on his face." She swooned. "Lukus's teeth shined white like school house chalk."

Years fell from Creola as she talked about her young love. "Dance, how he could dance! Lord, how we could cut the rug!"

"You cut up a rug?"

"No, child! Lord, have mercy! 'Cuttin' the rug' means dancing wild and crazy and real fast."

"I know how you can dance!"

"That's right, Miss Moonbeam. So now you understand that you are learning to 'cut the rug,' too."

I grinned. "Sure do!"

Creola seemed to go off for a moment into a world of her own dreams.

I peered at her. "What ever became of Lukus?"

Creola's face drained of all light. Life vanished from her eyes. Her sweet and happy smile twisted into a wounded frown.

"Dead. My Lukus is buried up by the church house."

I took her hand. Couldn't say a word. I didn't have a glimmer about what to do to console her. My eyes filled with tears.

She clucked her tongue. "Miss Moonbeam, it's all right. Fact is, many years washed clean my hurt. I'll be myself directly. But, listen to me; we'll speak of this no more. Mine is not the story you need to know. After this morning, you must promise that you will never again mention Lukus."

"I promise." That summer morning, I understood Creola had shared with me a sacred trust.

"Now, Miss Moonbeam, listen carefully and look here."

She reached into her apron pocket. "Lukus gave me something before he passed. I've always wondered what to do with it. Now, I know. Last night, the Angel of Finding Things came to me in a dream. She hovered at the foot of my bed and gave me a message."

Creola handed me a tiny white box, one yellowed by time and worn from countless openings — and closings. "Go ahead. Open it. I'm giving to you."

Inside was a gold ring with two tiny hearts. "For me?"

"Of course, Miss Moonbeam." A single tear zigzagged down the wrinkles of her cheek. "The angel says it will hold the place until your amethyst comes back to us."

"Thank you, oh, thank you."

"My ring is way too big for your sweet hand right now. So I brought this chain with me. You can wear it around your neck 'til your finger grows bigger. Let's see how it looks."

"Oh Crellie, it's beautiful! Were these hearts for you and your friend?"

"Yes, but now they are for us, you and your Creola."

"Moonbeam and Crellie forever."

"That's right. It looks mighty pretty on you. Much better for my baby to wear it than for it to live forever in that box." With that she pitched the worn little box into a metal trash can.

I hugged her neck as we both admired the ring. "I almost hope I don't find my birthstone. I like your ring much better. Oh, Crellie, thank you!"

"Precious child, should we find your ring, we'll simply say that you are a two-ring moonbeam."

When Mary Pearle got home from camp, we told her that we got the ring at Woolworth's to replace my birthstone and to cheer me up while she was away. My sister fell for that, hook, line and sinker!

That ring meant as much to me as any piece of jewelry I've ever received.

I kept it until the day Creola died.

CHAPTER 12

For the next two weeks I worked with vigor on my new Creola book. The days literally zipped by. That's what happens to me when I'm writing with my heart. It was as if Creola was urging me onward. Maybe she was? Maybe she was swooping about the condo with the Angel of Finding Things. I was certainly finding *myself.*

As always, Beau's three-day visit came and went all too quickly for me, for us. We agreed that I would never again plan a three-month stay away from home.

While Beau was there, we dropped by Sonny Gilmore's bookstore. My fears quieted as soon as I discovered there was no sale table with my books marked down to a dollar. Quite the contrary, Mr. Gilmore proudly pointed to his special display of Newberry novels, all of which were being sold at the regular retail price. To my delight, there was a vase of yellow roses in the middle of the book-filled table.

"Roses are my favorite, Mr. Gilmore, especially yellow ones."

"Been meaning to invite you over," he apologized. "I called in the order as soon as you went to Miss Eugenia's ice cream shop. I knew Eugenia would fix you up with a place to rent so you'd be spending the summer with us."

I turned to Beau. "Everyone around here seems to anticipate my decisions well before I make them."

"Wish I had that knack."

"I just bet you do."

He gave me a squeeze. I grinned at Mr. Gilmore. "Your display flatters me. Thank you."

"You're welcome. Please call me Sonny."

"Please call me Honey." Beau cleared his throat. "Oh, excuse me, darling. Sonny, I want to introduce my husband. This handsome man is Beau, Beau Newberry."

"Pleased to meet you, Beau." He extended his hand. "We've already sold a good many of your wife's books. I hope she'll autograph the ones we've got left."

I nodded. "I brought my pen. This is the one I use exclusively for special events."

"Now, *I'm* flattered, Mrs. Newberry, errr, Honey. I tried to locate all your books. Got every one of them, too, except for that *'Spinster's Petticoat.'* Then I finally found it, too. Lucky for me, a feller in Orlando spotted one at an estate sale. Beatrice has folks passing it around. 'Course I'd like it better if they were spending their money in my store."

"Hope the guy paid more than a dollar for it," teased Beau.

I kicked at him.

Saturday night, Beau and I had dinner at our favorite spot at the marina. On Sunday, Beatrice joined us for steaks at the condo. She and Beau hit it off like two old friends. When she was getting ready to leave, she gave Beau a kiss on his lips and commented, "If I were two decades younger, Honey, I'd give you a run for your money with this charming man."

"Well, I'm not so sure I feel very comfortable about Beau driving you home."

"You're a smart woman, Honey."

Beau winked at me as he escorted Beatrice to the car. "I'll try to be home by daybreak."

At the end of the weekend it was sad for me to watch as my husband drove from the parking lot. I went back inside the condo, slumped in a chair, and gobbled a still-warm biscuit. "Rally, girl, you have to rally."

My battle cry worked. By midmorning, I resolutely jumped feet first into *Creola's Moonbeam.* Besides, I had to justify renting the condo.

A few days later, pleased with the progress, I telephoned my editor.

"Guess what I'm doing?"

"Windsurfing?"

"No! I'm writing a book, one you'll surely beg me to publish."

"Hmmm, maybe you should try the windsurfing thing."

"Uh oh, you're cranky. Are you dieting again?"

"No, I'm kidding. I'm pleased you are back at work. Good luck, Honey, and *hurry!*"

"What, already a deadline? Some things never change!"

I looked for Beatrice on the beach the next morning. Sadly, the lady was not there. I took a second walk near sunset, thinking my friend had changed her schedule. I was not so busy that I didn't have time to be concerned about her. Finally, I went by her cottage and knocked on the door. There was no answer.

I peeked through the window. There was no sign she was home, only her collections of beautiful pieces tempted me to come inside. Walking around peering into her windows proved to me that my friend was nowhere to be found.

I'd sent my short stories to her on a disc, so she could read them on her computer. It occurred to me that my stories were so pathetic that Beatrice had run away to avoid telling me the truth. I'd had reservations about them since the day I tossed the printed manuscript in our garbage.

Creola tsked-tsked in my thoughts. *Don't be ridiculous, Moonbeam. They weren't that bad.*

My fears about Beatrice's critique quickly turned into a gnawing feeling that something was wrong, not with my work, but with Beatrice.

The truth surfaced two days later. A postcard arrived from Atlanta.

My dear Honey,

I'm in the hospital from laughing too hard at your stories. The flamingos! The roofers! The POOL! I read the story about the cock-eyed paper hanger and am still trying to recover. The poor daft fellow hung your striped paper horizontally and explained the problem was because your house, as he put it, "just ain't squaar." Guffawing so, I must have broken some ribs!

How about the one where Beau floods the entire first floor trying to unclog the kitchen sink with a garden hose! That doesn't sound like the capable man I've just met!

I will return on Monday.

Love, Beatrice

Beatrice in the hospital? I couldn't describe my feelings. I pinned a note to her door and anxiously awaited her return.

Two days later, the phone rang. It was Beatrice. "Did you get my postcard?"

"Yes, but, Beatrice, I can't help but be worried about you. Please tell me what's wrong."

"Deary me, my poorly chosen jest about the hospital alarmed you. Forgive me, Honey. Besides, what could possibly be wrong with this old dame? Lest you forget, I once drank from the Fountain of Youth."

"Guess that slipped my mind. I'm thrilled to hear your voice."

"Good, but, dear girl, why is it that you haven't gotten these charming stories into print?"

"Apparently, Beatrice, you're more confident about them than I am. Besides, I'm currently hard at work on Creola."

"Making progress, are you?"

"Yes, indeed, and loving every minute of the writing. I'm nearly finished with the first draft."

"Good for you, but about these other stories. They *are* simply marvelous."

"Maybe you like them because you've gotten to know me. They're very personal. Boring?"

"Hardly. Take the story about the fence as an example. Think how many people will relate to that one. And that one about the plumber and, ah hem, the *galvanized nipples.* That's an attention getter!"

I pooh-poohed my friend's praise and pleaded with her to allow me to come by. Beatrice, saying she remained worn out from her trip to Atlanta, begged off. Concerned more than ever, I reluctantly changed the subject.

"Did you visit Jennings?"

"Yes, of course. Although I didn't find a good opportunity to encourage him to visit *you* once you're back in that fearsome city. For that I apologize. At any rate, he and I had a grand holiday."

I was delighted that Beatrice was safely home in her beloved cottage. I was also pleased to learn she had enjoyed her Jennings.

Selfishly, I was equally thrilled with my friend's generous praise regarding the stories. Later that night, I put aside my new project and took a look at the story Beatrice commented on regarding the plumber.

Lady, You've Got Galvanized Nipples

BY HONEY NEWBERRY

"Sorry to interrupt your meeting, ladies," said Russell Long as he leaned into the sunroom. "Mrs. Newberry, I'm afraid Bobby and I have found something you'll probably wanna see."

Doubt that. "Of course."

"The news isn't good, Mrs. Newberry. Come back here and we'll explain what's going on."

Rising apprehensively from the wicker chair, I fretfully ran my fingers through my newly cut, currently blond hair. My clattering teacup's frenetic clicking on the saucer confirmed a mounting level of anxiety.

"It seems these nice men need a *quick* word with me," I chirped hopefully to the women of my writer's group. A manuscript slid off my lap, its pages dispersed throughout the sunroom like paper napkins in a burst of summer wind. "I'll be right back."

I didn't want to hear bad news from my

plumbers. My body's temperature rose as my neck began to constrict. I suffer from plumbing phobia, which is something akin to one's apprehension upon going to a periodontist's office. As we entered the bathroom, my gums began to feel tender. They were puffy, too. I ran my tongue around my mouth. "Hmmm, blood? Maybe not. Maybe I'm just drooling."

"What's that?" asked Russell.

"Oh, just thinking out loud."

He pointed to his assistant, Bobby. "Let's start by discussing the situation here in the main bathroom."

"Sure," said I with forced self-confidence. Their tag-team approach intimidated me all the more. The three of us squatted down and wedged our bodies halfway into the bathroom cabinet. I bumped my head. We were down on our knees, shoulder-to-shoulder, heads burrowed together so we were nearly nose-to-nose.

Russell pointed his flashlight at the area in question. Shaking his head, he sighed deeply and began, "See where your pipe goes into your wall there?"

"Yes, I see."

Bobby nodded in agreement.

Russell sighed. "I'm sorry to tell you this. See, you've got these galvanized pipes, so naturally, your nipples are galvanized, too."

"What?" Again, I bumped my head. I started to giggle. "Did you say something about, eerrrr, nipples?" My face grew hot.

"Your house was constructed in the early 1960's. The pipes were made from lead."

"Not a good thing," I surmised.

They continued on patiently talking to me, giving me more detail than I could possibly comprehend. Still, I paid close attention, wondering when they'd explain about nipples. In their concluding statement, the plumbers noted that the lead pipes were attached to the wall with a round piece called "the nipple."

Ah-hah.

"Look right here, Mrs. Newberry, that's your nipple. See it?"

"Um huh. Nipple."

"That's where you folks got your problem."

That was what I *heard.* What I *saw* was nasty rust and a good bit of cruddy gunk. Little wonder we had only a tiny trickle coming from that faucet. I shuddered to think about the condition of the water we were using to brush our teeth. Were my gums really bleeding? Perhaps they were actually *rusting.*

I replied astutely, "Yuk."

"The job's gonna take a good bit of time."

"Umm, huh, time," said I. *Time,* as any homeowner knows, is the international code word for *money.*

Bobby, Russell, and I extricated ourselves from under the cabinet.

"The job will call for new materials, of course, and then there'll have to be a good bit of drilling and ripping out before we can start."

Translation: we'd have noise and mess along with the significant outlay of money.

Some customers, most *normal* customers, would have panicked. The me-of-old would have dissolved into tears, but, because we had battled this house for such a long time, this type of announcement had become a way of life.

I rolled my shoulders and cracked my neck. "No problem."

"Sorry again about this news, ma'am. I'm afraid there's more."

"Let me have it."

We passed by the sunroom en route to the basement. I called to my writers' group, "It will be another minute or two, girls."

"Go ahead, we've gone on without you," one called back.

I smiled, only faintly though.

Once in the basement, I pointed out the

water spots on the ceiling tiles. I flipped on the light switch. With that, the just replaced bulbs began to sizzle and hiss. "There, you see," I said, "water spots."

Russell whipped out his flashlight and aimed it at the ceiling. With his index finger, the plumber poked a hole in the tile and immediately jumped backwards. I wasn't nearly as quick, so I got dusted from head to toe with a white, powdery substance.

"Whoops, sorry 'bout that, ma'am. I didn't expect that much fallout."

"No problem."

Even Bobby was surprised. He, too, had to dust himself off.

I looked at him. "Not a good sign, is it?"

"The shower pan, Mrs. Newberry, it's the shower pan all right."

"What's a shower pan?"

The tag-team answered in unison. "It's the bottom of your shower, ma'am."

A future scene flashed before me.

6:45 a.m. Beau stands in the shower.

6:55 a.m. Steam rises, his shampoo bubbles. His eyes blink open as he wipes water droplets from his lovely brown lashes.

7:00 a.m. There comes a rumble, then a cracking sound as the shower floor begins to quake. A terrified shriek and my beloved crashes through the ceiling onto the basement floor. The shampoo bottle remains gripped firmly in Beau's lifeless hand. I foresee myself dialing 911.

I looked at Russell and Bobby without a shred of hesitation and said, "Fix it."

I quickly ushered the men upstairs and into the room where my writers' group was finishing up. "Ladies, I want to introduce our favorite plumbers to you. Russell and Bobby, this is Beverly, Janet, Lalor, Dorothy, and our second Janet."

The girls each responded with "Hello's" and "Nice to meet you's."

The men answered, "How y'all doin'?"

I looked at my friends dully. "I'm afraid we'll have to host a telethon to pay for this."

They uttered sympathetic "Oh no's" and "Dear me's."

Russell shrugged his shoulders and laughed nervously. "Well, we hope it won't be *that* bad, Mrs. Newberry."

"Oh, yes, it will be." I put my hand on each of the plumbers' backs. "Ladies, it seems I have galvanized nipples."

At first, there was a collective gasp, then their tentative giggles burst into howls.

Russell stammered, "Well, g-guess we gotta go. Come on, Bobby."

I escorted them out. Russell called back to me as he got in his truck, "I'll let you know when I can line up the shower pan man." Cranking the vehicle, Russell looked at Bobby, shook his head, and took off.

I slouched back inside. "Y'all are rats deserting a sinking ship!" I teased as my friends prepared to leave. They hooted. I followed them outside and watched them climb merrily into their cars.

Janet rolled down her window and attempted to say something, but all she could muster was another snicker. She rolled up the window and backed down the driveway. I could see her head bobbing as she made her way to the end of the street.

I went to the phone and called Beau. He was awaiting the plumbers' estimate. Somewhere in the ballpark of thirty-five dollars upwards to a hundred, he'd decided. I tried to lighten the moment, so I described the girls' reactions.

He didn't see one iota of humor. Like most husbands, Beau doesn't share his wife's idea of what's funny.

After I finished reading the nipple story, I cut up a bowl full of fresh fruit. Fruit would provide balance for all the cheese crackers I was currently consuming. The downside of writing, for me, is how badly it impacts my generally well-balanced diet. This is especially the case when Beau is not around.

It's too much trouble for me, as a focused writer, to eat anything but quick, crunchy meals. "Quick" accommodates my schedule while "crunchy" takes care of my stress. Just under ten pounds per book is proof positive that the quick and crunchy diet isn't a good one. Even so, I'm more content while writing stories than I am when eating wisely.

I sat back down at my computer. I'd intended to read just one of the stories that I'd given to Beatrice. However, I came upon another favorite, "The Dog Fort" and couldn't resist. Apparently, it's one Beatrice liked, too. Once again, Creola had to simmer on the back burner.

I'll be waiting, she whispered.

THE DOG FORT

BY HONEY NEWBERRY

Champ, the collie dog who lived in the house behind ours, truly enjoyed the sound of his own bark. But he was selective in his choice of "barkee."

Champ barked only at Beau.

One neighbor finally confided in us that the teenage boy who had lived in our house prior to us often antagonized the otherwise calm dog. It was becoming apparent that Champ believed my husband was that young man.

Each and every time Beau went outside, Champ snarled, barked feverishly, and tried to leap his chain length fence. However, should any other member of our family go outside, even venturing all the way up to his fence, Champ would wag his tail gleefully.

The problem escalated to such a level that the dog would go into a frenzy should he as much as spot Beau in our sunroom. This was beginning to bother my husband. Every afternoon, when he came home from work, his appearance would spark Champ's frenzied barking. Beau's reactions also were beginning to escalate, as well.

One particular day stands out in my memory. Same drill: Beau drove up and got out of the car. Champ stood poised at his fence, his head erect, his eyes sharp, teeth bared. The barking began.

It was then that Beau snapped. He grabbed a yard rake. Running through the back yard, headed for Champ, he screamed at the top of his lungs and whirled the rake over his head in the style of a rotating helicopter blade.

Neighbors gathered laughing and cheering him on as my husband, grasping a rake, charged like Mel Gibson in *Braveheart.* "Champ, you son of a —" He stopped and hurled the rake at the dog.

The rake missed. Champ barked all the louder.

So did Beau.

Mrs. Whitmere, a quiet, unassuming lady who lived next door to Champ, shouted out her window, "For goodness sakes, Beau, you're making more noise than the dog!"

Somewhat embarrassed, my husband muttered back to her, "Sorry about that, Mrs. Whitmere."

Unlike Mel Gibson, he retreated.

Although Champ's afternoon ritual continued even after the rake incident, Beau tried to temper his reactions. Oh, the change was not all together due to Mrs. Whitmire's remark. Beau had thrown several other expensive tools at Champ, and he wasn't comfortable about asking his owners to return them. Beau resorted to making a wee-hours-of-the-morning telephone call.

3:30 a.m. "Hello, George!"

"Hello?" yawned Champ's owner.

A pause. Then came Beau's loud "RRR-ROOOOFFFFFFFF, RRROOFF!" For added drama, he slammed down the phone.

I sat up in bed and crossed my arms. "Beau, aren't you ashamed?"

Beau pounded his pillow and grunted. "Nope."

One Saturday morning, Champ escaped from his yard, into ours. Would he finally get a nose-to-snout look at his human antagonist? The dog stopped for a quick drink of chlorinated water from our pool and lost his footing. Beau and I were working in the front yard when we heard the commotion. We raced toward the sounds of splashing and frantic yelping.

"Good grief!" I yelled. "Champ's drowning!"

The water was weighing down his heavy, collie coat. In his panic, the frightened animal couldn't find his way to the steps.

It's also significant to explain that it was the fall of the year and rather chilly. Even so, Beau didn't hesitate. My heroic husband jumped in, swam to the dog, and pulled him to safety.

His teeth chattering, Beau stomped up our back steps and went inside to change out of his wet clothes. As I applauded wildly, Champ ran home. Later, I related the story to the children of how their Daddy had saved Champ's life.

The kids decided their dad was a hero. His actions, in my view, were comparable to Captain Ahab resuscitating Moby Dick.

Mary Catherine made note of that and questioned him. "Daddy, I thought you hated that dog?"

Beau sighed. "Still do."

The estimate to build an eight-foot wooden fence around our entire back yard came to 8,000 dollars. Beau went for it. A couple of days later, a truck arrived with the lumber. Or, should I say, the *first* truck arrived. There would be several deliveries. This fence was to become the Newberry's very own Fort Apache. Still and all, the fence would silence that dog.

"Worth any expense," reasoned Beau.

Rick Hogg, our builder, asked if we'd object were he to bring along his dog, Heidi. "It's just such a nice day, I hate to lock her up when she could be outside playing."

"Of course, it'll be fun to have her," I agreed.

Heidi, a mixed-breed terrier, leapt gleefully out from Rick's truck. She scampered around, circling her master every step of his way.

"Calm down, girl."

Heidi obliged and quietly continued to make herself at home. The curious pup checked out every inch of our backyard as, one by one, she sniffed each tree and bush.

The kitchen door at Champ's home opened. He advanced onto his porch. His ears perked. Champ sprung from the top stoop. Charging toward Heidi, he erupted in a vicious, "RRRRooooooolllllllf!" His reaction to the visiting dog rivaled any he had shown toward Beau.

Heidi was taken aback. She stiffened, then burst forward, charging like a hungry lion. She screeched to a stop at Champ's chain-link fence. Nose to nose. Heidi growled.

Champ growled back. Heidi barked. Champ tucked his tail, turned around, and quietly slinked up to his porch.

Heidi triumphed as the champion of the two beasts.

Rick shook his head. "Looks like you didn't need an expensive fence after all. Heidi works for dog biscuits."

THE BOMB SCARE

BY HONEY NEWBERRY

When Beau and I moved into our Atlanta neighborhood in April of 1982, we were one of the first families to come along with young children in more than a decade. What a disruptive force our family must have been to the formerly peaceful neighborhood of retired people.

At one neighbor man's funeral, I suddenly felt an urge to apologize to his widow for all the trouble my family caused in those early years. Was mine a need for absolution? Most assuredly.

There has rarely been any extended time of peace and tranquility around the Newberry household. The following incident is a typical example of our singular brand of havoc.

Beau was on his way home from work one quiet spring afternoon when he turned onto our street and noticed a large crowd gathering at the top of our hill. Not only were there police cars, there was a van from *the bomb squad!*

"What in the *world?"* Beau pulled halfway into the garage, slammed on his breaks, and raced inside to make sure his family was all right. There he found a note from me:

> Please drive the soccer carpool at 5:30. Mary Catherine's at school, and I'm at a PTA board meeting. We should get home in time for dinner. I'll pick up Chinese.
>
> Love you, Honey

"Whew, that's a relief. Thank goodness that Honey and the children are safe."

Children? Wait a minute. My note only accounted for our daughter. Not our son.

Beau's eyes opened wide. Actually, my husband vows that his pupils literally *dilated* from shock when he suspected, beyond a shadow of a doubt, that our son Butlar and his band of ten-year-old buddies had something to do with the emergency. He raced up the street, where he found Fulton County firefighters, police officers, paramedics, and detonation experts swarming our neighbor's home.

"What's going on?"

"I don't know," replied Cantey, our neighbor. "We heard the sirens about fifteen minutes ago. Wylda and I ran over to see what all the excitement was about."

"What do y'all make of the Bomb Squad truck?" asked another man.

Beau just shook his head.

Our frantic neighbor, Bruce, came through his back gate and joined the group. The father of two preschool girls, he was trembling, and his face was as white as the sand in his daughters' sandbox.

"I can't t-tell you much," stammered Bruce. "I was digging a hole for a rosebush, and *ka-plunk,* my shovel struck something hard. I figured it was just a rock until I bent down to pitch it out of my way. The thing looks just like a hand grenade!"

The crowd gasped.

"I called 911 for the fire department. They're back there now. I expect the bomb squad will have to take whatever it is away from here and blow it up."

Murmurs of "blow it up" echoed through the crowd.

"For the life of me, I can't imagine how such a dangerous thing got into my yard!"

Beau moved closer toward Bruce. "I should take a look at what you've found."

"Don't try to be a hero, Beau. That thing might explode and blow you to Kingdom

Come! I think we all should stay right where we are. For safety's sake, you do understand."

Beau found the officer in charge. He whispered something to the man and the two went around to the back of Bruce's house. Once there, he saw six or eight men gathered around a box. In the company of the fire chief, my husband ventured closer. Whatever the object was, the bomb squad was being extremely cautious with it. One man gently placed the device in the box while another carefully packed it in some protective material.

Beau finally got a good look. His face turned as red as the fire trucks parked out front.

"Damn."

"What, sir?"

"Ummm, let me see that thing." With that, Beau reached down and picked up the box. The bomb squad men leapt back, dropped to the ground, and covered their heads. Other emergency people scattered.

"Look out!"

"Man, are you nuts?"

Beau stood calmly holding the object out for a captain to peruse. The captain stared at it then groaned with disgust. "It's okay, men. The excitement's all over." He glowered at Beau. "I suppose the good news is that there never was any real danger here."

My poor husband, still beet red, uttered, "I don't know what to say. I really am sorry about this."

"It happens," said the captain. "Okay, folks, we've eliminated the problem. Everything's fine and everyone can go home now."

Puzzled, maybe a little annoyed that "whatever" turned out to be nothing at all, the neighbors returned home to dinner, to television, to phone calls, and to reading the evening paper. To our knowledge, no one ever discovered exactly what Bruce dug up in his garden.

And no one in the Newberry family was ever going to tell them.

When I got home, Beau was talking with Butlar. I caught a few words. It was one of those father-son discussions that I knew was best left to them. I set the table and opened the takeout boxes of Chinese food.

Beau shared the truth with me later that night. Several months prior, Beau had taken Butlar and his buddies, Ben, Jeffrey, and Casey, on an adventure to their favorite haunt, the Army Navy surplus store. The guys begged Beau for some of those cool-as-could-be "practice" grenades. He'd reluctantly agreed to purchase a few of the "dummies" so they could play "war" in *our* back yard. The key phrase being in *our* back yard.

Apparently, one of the dummies found its way into the yard of the genteel man up the hill. War was not a familiar venue for Bruce. He was far more accustomed to watching his two little girls play on swing sets and have tea parties with their dolls.

Yes, Bruce, we will let you in on our secret, now. It was us. Actually, it was Butlar, with Beau's assistance. Mary Catherine and I are innocent of this particular transgression. If you and your family hadn't moved shortly thereafter, we'd gladly purchase extra boxes of those delicious Girl Scout cookies from your daughters.

In closing, and as always, the Newberry family would like to apologize to all of our neighbors and let them know that our children are grown and are currently living far, far away.

That evening when Beau called the beach condo, I brought up the bomb-scare incident.

"Isn't it curious that Bruce moved away right after that? Surely he wasn't that upset about the hand grenade."

"If you can't take the heat, you better get

236

out of the kitchen."

"For Pete's sakes, Beau, you can't mean that. Come to think of it, I really can't remember another time I saw him out in his front yard."

"Maybe Bruce was in his basement building a bomb shelter."

As Beau laughed at his own joke, I began to worry about our children's children, especially the males. How might they turn out?

"Beau, would you ever take one of our future grandsons to the Army Navy store?"

"Sure, why not?"

Beau Newberry definitely suffers from short-term memory loss.

CHAPTER 13

Her daughter's wedding behind her, Mary Pearle called and asked when she might come down for a few days.

"Tomorrow is good!" I told her. "Yes, come on, and hurry! Just make certain to bring some pictures from Susan's wedding. I can't wait to see them. Beau and I had such a wonderful time."

"That's marvelous to hear. I can't remember a thing. It's all a blur to this mother-of-the-bride."

"Well, believe me, Mary Pearle, you did yourself proud. Everything was perfection. Mary Catherine and Butlar are still raving about the band y'all had at the reception."

"Thank you, Honey. I'm about dead but it's a good dead."

"I've never seen my niece as happy. *And* was *she* ever gorgeous!"

"I almost can't believe Susan is mine. Her darling Matthew seems to adore my girl.

You know, I cannot bring myself to call that young man Susan's *husband.* They seem like babies to me."

"Don't you remember, Mary Pearle, Daddy didn't acknowledge you and I had husbands for years."

"You're right, I'd forgotten that. Daddy always wanted us to remain his little girls. By the way, to my great relief, Susan's father held up his end of the bargain. Edgar actually behaved himself."

"It was all I could do to acknowledge his presence, the selfish jerk. I think Beau had a few polite words with him."

"Forget Edgar. Let's talk about the beach. Now please don't go to a minute's trouble on my account. I only want to stare at the Gulf, drink water, and read."

"Don't worry about me distracting you. I'm really busy with this book. In fact, the weekend at the wedding provided just the right break for me. Now I'm back working constantly, and you know how that can be. I crunched through an entire bag of Jordan almonds for lunch and dinner yesterday. I will get up from my computer and give you a welcoming hug, but that's all I can promise."

"Perfect!"

■ ■ ■ ■

"Beatrice, I hope you will come over to meet my sister Mary Pearle. She's arriving on Tuesday."

"Glorious! But I insist we gather over here. I'll have a dinner party for the four of us, you and your sister, Oscar and me. The dear man has just come back from his trip to Africa and would love to regale us with tales from his safari."

"Are you quite certain you are up to company? This week you've seemed a bit under the weather."

"That's your all-too-active imagination at work again," growled Beatrice. "I'll not have you behaving in an impertinent way. I truly want to entertain your sister at my cottage."

I had been brought to my knees by the queen mother.

"Thank you, Beatrice. It'll be fun. I know Mary Pearle will be completely fascinated by you."

"Of course, she will be! My guests are rarely disappointed."

I got an idea. "Beatrice, you remember that my sister is divorced."

"Oh yes, been there, done that, dear."

"Well, I'm very worried about her, especially since her daughter's wedding is over. The planning kept her busy for weeks, and now she has very little to occupy her time. Mary Pearle is awfully forlorn now that both of her girls are out of her home."

"Poor dear. I'm glad she's coming to be with you. We'll boost her spirits, you'll see."

"Your friend Oscar sounds like a charming fellow. Do you think he might take an interest in her?"

"Oscar? Heavens no. That man is too old even for *me!*"

"Didn't you say he's just back from a safari?"

"So he says. Travel has nothing to do with age! Besides, don't you remember my telling you that Oscar must avoid the sun? I'm convinced the man remained in his tent the entire time. As well, Oscar would never consider shooting a gun, he's anti-NRA. I think the old boy was merely after fresh conversation for dinner parties."

"I assumed he was — oh, I'm embarrassed. I shouldn't try to matchmake."

"Don't fret! You were only being compassionate. Your sister, if she's even half as darling as you, deserves to find companionship. She's only experienced the one love? My lord, she's a novice!"

"A novice who's been wounded."

"All the more reason for the universe to send healing her way. I feel it in my bones, your Mary Pearle will find another."

"I hope you're right."

"In matters of the heart, I usually am. But, for now, let's settle our plans. We can work on your sister's romance once I get to know her."

I thanked my friend for the kind invitation and for her heartening comments. "Looks like you are always giving wise counsel to us Butlar girls. You're a later edition of our Creola."

"That's rare praise, indeed."

"Sincerely meant. Mary Pearle and I will make ourselves available any time that's convenient for you and Oscar. I do insist on bringing the dessert. I make a mean key lime pie."

"Rubbish. When I invite, I prepare."

On the way to the dinner, I gave my sister a bit of background. "Don't forget, Beatrice is rather eccentric, and I have no idea what Oscar will be like. You should be prepared for almost anything."

"Listen lady, I'm tickled pink that she's gotten you going on your book. My only disappointment is that I've just arrived. I wanted some time with my baby sister before meeting her friends."

"Beggars can't be choosers."

"I'm not complaining, Honey, this is really a grand welcome for me. And the dinner party is also serving to get you off the computer! I'm afraid you'll soon go blind from staring at that screen."

"I thought you were glad I was working again?"

"Okay, so I'm contradictory."

As we walked up to Beatrice's cottage, the door suddenly swung open. There stood Oscar in full safari dress.

"Welcome to Kenya. I am Oscar. I am your official guide for this evening." With that, the wizened, gray-haired Scottish gentleman stepped aside, and, extending his arm, motioned for us to enter.

Mary Pearle pursed her lips at me and whispered, "And heeeeerrre we go!"

"I told you to expect the unexpected."

All manner of strange smells wafted from the kitchen. Beatrice's usual array of books and objects of art remained scattered about but were complemented by photos of animals in the jungle, exotic plants, and huge African masks. A seven-foot stuffed python curled down from the chandelier and onto the dining room table.

Covered with bamboo, the table was set

sparsely with wooden bowls and a single ladle for each of the four diners. Stereo speakers, which ordinarily played classical music, squawked and hooted with the songs and sounds of tropical birds.

Oscar put a hand to his heart. "Would you ladies like a drink?"

"Yes, yes, please!"

Beatrice danced into the room. Dressed in colorful African fabric and wearing flowers atop her turban-wrapped hair, she began beating a large drum, which hung from her shoulder by a colorful strap.

"Welcome, friends, welcome to my country! I call it the Jungle of Mexico Gulf."

Everyone laughed.

"Don't laugh at me! My late husband, 'What's His Name,' and I played this very drum at a royal luau in Maui. It was a glorious experience. I do enjoy a good drum, don't you, Mary Pearle?"

I looked over at my sister. Mary Pearle's face was frozen into a toothy grin. I recalled my own surprise when first Beatrice turned the cartwheel. Tonight the woman had outdone herself.

"You are the Lady Mary Pearle, elder sister of Royal Princess Honeybee, I presume?"

"Well, ah, oh yes, I, I, I suppose I am,"

stuttered my suddenly dumbstruck sibling, the Lady Mary Pearle.

The meal was scrumptious, featuring some sort of delicious fish — Beatrice wouldn't say exactly what it was. I was afraid to ask. There were bananas and mangos, tabouli, and odd, sweet-tasting breads along with shrimp (Beatrice rarely served a meal without some form of shrimp).

For dessert, we were treated to a four-layer chocolate cake. As our hostess explained, "I deemed it appropriate to have a layer for each member of our delegation from the Jungle of Mexico Gulf."

"Chocolate cake, my darling?" questioned Oscar. "Your dinner was divine, but never once on my journey to Africa was I served chocolate cake."

"That's all the more reason for you to have it tonight, dearest!"

Our foursome enjoyed thick, rich coffee along with the dessert while Oscar regaled us with tales of the safari. Contrary to Beatrice's theory, the fellow did indeed leave his tent. He joked that he took more photographs "than there are animals in Africa."

"It's a shame I forgot to put film in my bloody camera!"

"Oh, Oscar," I groaned, "what a tragedy.

Tell you what, let's split a second piece of cake. It's often said that chocolate is the universal healing salve for all missed opportunities!"

Oscar agreed and happily took more cake, a whole piece.

"Count me in, too," echoed the Lady Mary Pearle.

Beatrice whispered in Oscar's ear.

"Guns, Beatrice? Of course not. There were no guns! We were a most civilized lot. The hunters in our party were only interested in capturing the animals on film. Blast me for being such an absentminded old duff!"

"Now, now, dear. It was more important that you had a superb time. Despite what they say, most people really aren't interested in other travelers' giraffes. Besides, you have those images burned in your mind's eye. How much more accessible is that than having to flip though an album?"

"Right you are, as always, my dear."

"What do you say we adjourn to more comfortable chairs?" suggested Beatrice. As we stood up, I insisted that I would host our next event. "I won't promise pythons and bird sounds, but I'll prepare my failsafe pork roast."

"Pork? Sounds like a luau to me," said

Beatrice. "I'll bring my drum and do a hula for you!"

Mary Pearle remarked, "I'll stay over for *that*. Beatrice, will you bring your chocolate cake?"

"Of course!"

My sister *hmmmed* as she licked the last drip of icing from her fingers.

I may never offer my key lime pie again.

Our after-dinner celebration became more serene as Mary Pearle was given an abbreviated tour of "The Queen Beatrice Gallery," my new term for Beatrice's enchanted cottage.

"Is it everything I said?" I whispered.

My sister, a mathematics teacher and not the emotionally involved art lover I am, nodded her appreciation. "And more, I can well see how spending time here has given rise to your creativity."

Beatrice lounged in her soft, comfortable chair, watching and savoring the praise of her Dear Ones' work, while Oscar saw to the dishes.

She called to him, "Do you feel demoted, Oscar?"

He waved his towel at her. "Not when I've had the pleasure of serving three such beautiful ladies."

"Scottish by blood, but Italian in his zest

for the female," declared Beatrice.

As we walked down the beach toward the condo, Mary Pearle went on and on about the evening, how much she enjoyed the company, the food, and, in particular, how much she enjoyed Beatrice and Oscar.

"They are quite a devoted couple, aren't they?"

"Couple? Oh heavens no! Those two have been friends for years. In fact, I suggested that Oscar, even though he's much your senior, could be an interesting man for you to date."

"What!"

"Yes, I did. A well-traveled and fascinating fellow like Oscar could be just what the doctor ordered for you."

"First of all, I'm totally mortified. Secondly, I wish you'd just mind your own business, Harriette Ophelia Butlar Newberry!"

"That was quite a mouthful, big sister."

"And was meant to get your attention, little sis."

"Don't get your panties in a wad. Beatrice stopped me right away, saying Oscar was even too old for *her*."

"I cannot believe you did that. It's a good thing you didn't tell me before I met him. I could just shoot you. Besides, I've already missed out on a great date with Oscar. He went on the safari without me."

"See, you *are* interested. It's not too late, you know."

"Oh, for Pete's sakes, quit."

"Spoil-sport!"

"Yeah, yeah. Dear sister, you really are fortunate, you do realize? Not everyone can marry a prince like Beau."

"Well, I can't wait to pass on that compliment."

"Don't you dare tell him. It's a sister thing, like the client–attorney privilege. Besides, your husband has more than enough ego already."

"Good, things sound back to normal."

"I'm glad you think so. Now, Honey, going back to my original comment about Beatrice and Oscar, I remain convinced they have some history that even *you* may have overlooked."

"I will admit one thing: Beatrice is full of surprises and mystery. Maybe you're right about her and Oscar. Bravo for you, Mary Pearle! I'll have to sharpen my perceptive skills next time we gather."

"Score one for my team. Tell you what, Honey, let's sit and watch the moon for a while and let that glorious meal try to digest itself. I do have something else on my agenda."

There was something in her tone that concerned me.

We settled into chaise lounges on the condo's balcony, cupping mugs of decaf coffee in our hands. Anyone seeing us from a distance — our shapes, our hair color, and mannerisms — could tell our obvious kinship. In the past, people occasionally mistook us for twins. Only recently had the well-earned lines on Mary Pearle's face given away our age difference. Mary Pearle's painful divorce, four years prior, had left its mark.

"Honey, I don't want you to get all in an uproar about this, but I *have* met someone."

I screamed, spilling decaf all over my lap and onto the chaise. The hot liquid splashed on her, too. We jumped up and ran inside for cold water and ice.

"Quick, the aloe plant."

We broke open a long stem and squeezed the healing gel onto my legs and her arm.

"That was some reaction, Royal Princess Honeybee."

"I'm sorry, are you all right?"

"The coffee hardly got on *me,* but how about *you?*"

"Your news was much more of a shock to

my system than was the decaf. Now, please tell me every single detail."

"His name's Stuart. He is smart and handsome enough, and very, very funny. And, by the way, he is ten years younger than me. We met on the Internet."

"The Internet! Mary Pearle, what are you thinking? Is this some kind of middle-age crisis?"

"It's the Internet factor that troubles you, isn't it?"

"For starters. The age difference got my attention, too. Mary Pearle, you have always had more sense than me. You were the one who made the best grades, who was class president, who got the great job right out of college."

"Lest you forget, I also married Edgar, who cheated on me from day one, and who, at almost sixty years of age, married *Bambi*."

"Her name is Bambi?"

"No, that's just what I'm currently calling the trashy teenage tart. She could be Bertha, for all I care."

"I didn't mean to go there, but please, please, let's just talk. You go first. I've got to get my head screwed back on. Begin with Stuart. I'd really like to know more about this man. Oh, Mary Pearle, you do know how much I love you and care about what happens to you?"

She hugged me. We sat back down on the lounges, and she began to talk. The moon drifted across the sky, reflecting into the sparkling Gulf waters and, it seemed, directly into Mary Pearle's eyes. The last years had been an especially long and painful journey for her, and I couldn't help but be concerned that she might be making another mistake.

The years of deceit, disappointment, and divorce had robbed Mary Pearle of every ounce of hope, joy, and confidence she once had in herself. On this night, however, her spunk and enthusiasm appeared to flow back into her as she spoke of her new man.

"Stuart has been like a balm for me. It's as if this man's love and attention have healed my wounds."

"He must be quite a guy. I can't tell you how glad I am that you came down to tell me about him in person."

"Stuart's suggestion."

"Two points for Stuart."

Mary Pearle filled me in on her impressive boyfriend; he was a widower with one grown son, an engineer. She and Stuart shared a passion for gardening, for golf, and, it would seem, for one another. The Internet-meeting part disturbed me, but the world had changed since my courting days. I'd have to adjust to that. For a while, it felt as if Mary Pearle and I were teenagers again, snuggled down in our twin beds in our parent's home, sharing secrets about boys.

Even so, the whole thing felt bizarre to me on several fronts. Beau and I had been uneasy about Mary Pearle and about her two daughters for a long time. We'd hoped that Mary Pearle's life would come together in the best possible way, but an Internet romance had never entered into our thoughts.

"You're being mighty quiet. Are you upset?"

"No, of course not, I'm still digesting."

"Dinner or my news?"

"Both."

Were I being honest with myself, I was disappointed that a chance meeting on the Internet had proven to be the magic potion for Mary Pearle. I was the bratty little sister, yes, but one who so much wanted to come up with the perfect man for her. I'd envisioned us as a quartet of friends, Beau, me, Mary Pearle and Mr. Wonderful. The only missing member was a boyfriend for Mary Pearle.

Maybe Stuart might become that man. Give

him a chance.

"Creola?"

Mary Pearle peered at me. "Did you say something, Honey?"

"No, not really."

"Are you sure your leg isn't badly burned?"

"No, it's fine, truly it is. The aloe, you know. I'm still in shock, that's all. So, when do we meet Prince Charming?"

"As soon as you like. We're getting married next month."

"*Mary Pearle,* have you gone completely insane?"

"I'm pregnant."

"What?"

"Just kidding. You remember, I had a hysterectomy."

"Very funny. Wait a second, while I get my heart started. Now, what do the girls think about this?"

"As you'd know, our daddy's girl, Katy, holds out hope that her father will come to his senses and put her family back together. Her sister, my clone, Susan, adores Stuart and plans to 'give me away' at the ceremony."

I flopped back on the lounge chair, nearly speechless.

Life goes on, Creola whispered.

■ ■ ■ ■

We talked on and on through the night. By the end, I was cautiously optimistic about my sister's astonishing announcement. Mary Pearle settled back on her lounge in happy silence. I changed the subject so we could both take a breather.

As every mother understands, I love to talk about my children. That I did. Aunt Mary Pearle was duly impressed. Of course, I was also all too happy to talk about my book, too. As I went into detail, my sister was equally elated.

"*Creola's Moonbeam is* a story worth writing, Honey."

"It's our story, too. Yours and mine. Mother's and Daddy's, as well. I don't think I could have written this while Creola was alive. She would have fought it every word of the way. Never liked being in the spotlight, did our Crellie."

"True."

"Even so, I wish she were here to enjoy it."

"Me, too."

I got up, went to my desk and returned with a stack of pages. "Here. Read this."

"What is it?"

"The story of Crellie's funeral."

THE FUNERAL

BY HONEY NEWBERRY

I thought back to the day of Creola's funeral. She'd died peacefully, in her sleep. Mary Pearle rode to the church with Beau and me while her kids and ours, Creola's four "grandchildren," followed behind in Butlar's car.

In an attempt to brighten my mood, Beau suggested that our beloved nanny might have kept herself alive until after Mary Pearle's divorce was final. "I expect Creola wanted to know for sure that her oldest baby was finally free of 'Edgar the Tomcat!' "

"You could be right, dear. I just hope Crellie will come back to haunt him!"

"Good Lord, Honey, can you imagine that?" said Mary Pearle. "I can see our Crellie now, her angel wings fluttering as she floats across the ceiling over that jerk and his mistress. Why, the sight of her ghost might give him a heart attack!"

"Mary Pearle! That's awful," I said, feigning horror and fanning myself with a hankie. "I'm certainly relieved that our four innocent children are riding in a separate car and not listening to your ravings!"

"You started it."

"Beau did."

"Now, now, Butlar girls," joked Beau, "please try to control yourselves."

"Yes, *Daddy*."

"Seriously, ladies, we're almost there."

The instant of frivolity plunged like a boulder into a river when we parked in the gravel lot beside Creola's church. I spotted the open pit of a freshly dug grave. Oh, God. It hit me that Mary Pearle and I had come to say goodbye to our second mother. First Daddy, then we'd lost Mother, now Creola.

It began to drizzle. Like my own heart, the air felt unbearably heavy. Everyone, every *thing* surrounding me was in mourning. We walked slowly inside. The seven of us — Mary Pearle, Beau, Mary Catherine, Butlar, Susan, Katy, and I — sat together, filling the pew in the tiny wooden hall of worship. Voices whispered. We were the only whites there.

"Those be Creola's people," someone whispered behind us. We met, for the first time, Creola's extended family. Her parents were long gone, but there were several cousins with older children and their own young.

The old darling had provided specific funeral instructions for her service. She insisted that the Butlar girls and their families be seated right up front near her "favorite" cousins, who knew well who we were.

"Look here," a cousin told us, handing me Creola's handwritten notes. She'd amended her original wishes as soon as I informed her about Mary Pearle's divorce. Sure enough, Creola's new funeral-seating instructions no longer included the line, *"with the exclusion of that devil Edgar that my Mary Pearle so unfortunately, and against my advice, married."*

I got up and went to her coffin, reaching in to gently caress her snow-white hair. I slipped the ring with two hearts — the one she'd presented me as a little girl, the ring I wore for so long on a chain — I slipped it into the pocket of her soft, lavender-flowered dress.

"I'm returning your ring, my dear Crellie. Be sure to have it on your finger when your beau of so long ago greets you by Heaven's gate. Perhaps he'll take you fishing in that place where death cannot separate God's good people." I struggled to quiet my emotions. "Cut a rug, Crellie, cut a rug."

The preacher eulogized this fine, gentle woman of enduring faith as the congregation again and again echoed a resounding "Amen." We clapped as he called upon the saints in heaven to welcome her home.

"Amen."

We raised our hands in praise for her long, hard, and generous life.

"Amen."

It seemed as if Creola were being carried straight to Heaven as the choir's singing of "Blessed Redeemer" and "Amazing Grace" all but lifted the tin roof right off the tiny church.

Broken-hearted, I sobbed into my husband's shoulder throughout the service.

After the burial, I walked among the other graves. Mystically drawn to an old tombstone, I was stunned to read the name.

Lukus "Fish" Jones.

"She's on her way," I whispered. "You'll know her, Lukus. Creola is young, she's beautiful, she's dancing toward you, and she's wearing your ring."

Creola left personal notes to Mary Pearle and to me. A cousin slipped mine into my purse as we hugged goodbye. She wrote words of love and encouragement and concluded with a poignant message:

"My Moonbeam, one day, I pray will be many, many years from now, you will find me in Heaven. I will be the strong pecan tree, planted right next to the Pearly Gates. Look for my leaves for they will be the many colors of autumn.
I love you most dearly, Creola"

Now, I finally shared the note with Mary Pearle. My sister wept.

"I always keep it in my purse," I told her. "I want to have Crellie's words with me wherever I go. It's like carrying a prayer card. For me, it's a blessed talisman, one I can touch for courage and strength."

Mary Pearle and I hugged.

CHAPTER 14

The next morning, we sat in the living room on a cozy, rattan sofa as I talked more about my new book. I explained that *Creola's Moonbeam* would chronicle events about the Butlar family and share a few of Creola's own stories. "It'll include tales of ghosts, funny anecdotes, and fables that she made up to teach us about life. I'll also fashion fictional accounts of Creola's family, as seen through the imaginations of us sisters."

Mary Pearle nodded. "I really love your idea, Honey. I'm so proud of you! Truly I am, but I also must confess, there've been times when I was jealous of your writing."

"You were jealous of *me?* I was always jealous of *you,* especially the fact that you were older. It infuriated me to realize I'd never be able to catch up. You got to go to camp first. Have boyfriends first. Get your driver's license first."

"But now, our two-year difference turns

out to be a good thing for you, wrinkle-wise."

"You're not looking close enough. But, Miss Mary Pearle, we both realize *you* got the best name."

"Yep, I know that. Poor Aunt Mary Pearle, though. She ended up going off the deep end. Didn't Mother ever tell you?"

"No, she didn't!"

Living up in New York and totally absorbed in her career, Aunt Mary Pearle had completely lost touch with her Southern roots, including touch with her brother and his family, even with her namesake, my sister.

Mary Pearle leaned closer, as if we still had to be discreet. "Well, you do understand how our mother felt. She always opted to take the high road when it came to family gossip."

"Even so, I have a right to find out what happened. Aunt Mary Pearle 'went off the deep end'? What on earth does that mean?"

"Mary Pearle Butlar Armstrong joined a commune!"

"A commune!" My brain was about to explode. I'd had entirely too many surprises for one twelve hour period of time.

"Seriously. Our aunt, the career woman extraordinaire, got involved with one of those wacko religious movements. Having retired early from her clothing company, she was looking for something interesting to occupy herself. She certainly found it! Aunt Mary Pearle met her 'guru' at a cocktail party, and before she knew what hit her, she'd signed over her apartment to him and moved into a group home with fifty or sixty of his disciples."

"I couldn't write a book this weird. Nobody would believe such a tale."

Mary Pearle went on to explain that our aunt had simply dropped off the planet. After many attempts to reach his sister, our father finally received a short letter from her. In it, Mary Pearle Armstrong made amends, saying she'd found her inner peace and would write again. Sadly, she never did. Not long after, our parents began facing their own battles with failing health.

The link vanished.

"It's tragic when a family simply fades away. Maybe —"

I hesitated. I must have looked especially forlorn. Mary Pearle eyed me worriedly. "Okay, lady, what are you thinking?"

"Nothing really, I'm just sad to find out about Aunt Mary Pearle. Wonder if she's still alive?"

"Honey Newberry, I can see what you are

doing. Stop! Leave well enough alone!"

"All right, big sister, for now I will. Fact is, I've already got way too much on my plate, anyway. Plate? Say, let's go out and get some breakfast. Seems you and I have talked the sun up."

"Are you sure we can eat again after all that food last night?"

"You know we can."

My waffle was practically floating in maple syrup.

"Aunt Mary Pearle gave away everything she had and moved into a commune," I said, shaking my head. "My sister is getting married to a younger man she met on the Internet."

"Actually, it was through a *dating* service on the Internet."

"Attention, everyone, my sister *is* officially crazy, just like our, eerrrr, *her* aunt! Tell me, Mary Pearle, what would Crellie be saying to you about your new boyfriend, emphasis on the 'boy'?"

"I think she's rejoicing. She's not as narrow-minded as you, and likely approves of Stuart's youth!"

"Whoops, sorry about that. You nailed me good."

"You're forgiven. Can I have a bite of your waffle?"

"Sure." I mimicked Creola's sweet, soft voice, "Priceless Pearlie, you are being guided in many ways. Best be paying mind, because someone could be calling to you on this very day. The spirit could be calling to you from deep inside . . . deep down inside your laptop computer! The Angel of the Internet speaks her wisdom."

"Blasphemy, Honey, you know Creola wasn't high tech, she would only come to us in a dream."

"Mary Pearle, you just might be surprised at the many ways Crellie can communicate!"

I couldn't wait to tell Beau the news. First, there was silence. Then his laughter. "Sounds like a plot for one of your books, Honey. You know, you'd introduce two brand new characters, 'the Mary Pearles.' You could call it, 'The Batty Bats in the Butlar Bell Tower!' "

"Good one, Beau."

"Pretty clever, if I do say so myself."

"Okay, okay, let's not allow this to go to your head. In all seriousness, I must tell you that it's been years since I've seen Mary Pearle this jubilant. Of course, I'm uneasy, but I'm also very happy for her."

"You don't think she's lonely, desperate even?"

"You sound like me, at first. No, I don't. She and I talked all night long. I'm afraid she's not only convinced herself, but she's convinced me, as well. In fact, she's bringing Stuart down to the condo in two weeks."

"I'll be there, Honey, in my role as big brother-in-law."

"I was counting on that."

I am well aware of my husband's keen ability to size up people. So often I make an acquaintance, introduce that person to Beau, and he'll warn me to be careful. He rarely makes a mistake. Somehow, knowing that weekend was coming, I relaxed and enjoyed the last days of Mary Pearle's visit.

Her secret revealed, Mary Pearle settled down, too. We were able to devote our attention to the Creola book.

It is always amazing to me that two people can remember things that happen in opposite ways. Identical event, same family, totally different version of same; it boggles my mind.

Mary Pearle and I delighted in the memory of a most special tea party, one which Creola orchestrated when we were around seven and nine years old. *My* memory included homemade cookies and a bus ride to the park with Creola hauling a child's folding table and three chairs to the shade of a big oak tree. I vividly recalled carrying a two-handled picnic basket filled with the cookies, paper cups and linen napkins, and lemonade in a thermos.

"No, that wasn't it at all," argued Mary Pearle. "The awful bus ride was to get the cookies at a fancy bakery. The tea party was in our own backyard. I can't believe you forgot. It was about the only time we didn't help Creola bake the cookies. Don't you remember, neither of us realized that you could actually buy cookies at a store?"

"The party was in our yard?" I was astounded. "The setting seemed so much more magical than our yard."

"That's because Creola hung Mother's prettiest sheets on the clothes line — pink ones, some yellow with flowers. Remember, you and I had to find our way through the billowy fairyland to 'Creola's Magic Garden Tea Room.' "

"Yes!" I admitted, "You're right. And she brought those funny old hats from her home!"

"Hats?"

"Hats. Mine was white with a gigantic gardenia."

"You're right! Creola wanted you to look

like the moon; you know, Creola's little Moonbeam. What was mine?"

"Yours, hmmm? Wait, I know! Priceless Pearlie wore purple. All 'P's!' It was a big, floppy hat with a lavender band covered in tiny seed pearls for 'Pearlie.' No detail was left undone."

"How could I forget something like that? See, little sister, we need *both* of our memories to write Creola's book. How I would love a picture of us with her on that day."

"How I would relish having *any* picture of Creola for this book. But then, maybe not. A memory can certainly be more mystical and intriguing than any ordinary snapshot."

In the end, Mary Pearle and I concurred on the details of the afternoon. Years melted like sugar cubes in the party's hot tea. To us, the most endearing feature of the occasion was our darling Creola's imagination, her sense of fun, and her love and devotion for us. We sisters knew our parents adored us, but it was Creola who was our Fairy Godmother.

I decided to dedicate my novel to Creola and Mary Pearle. I would give my sister her own acknowledgement for the story's writing, but that would remain a secret until its publication.

As we packed Mary Pearle's things the

night before she was to leave, I exclaimed, "Good heavens, Mary Pearle, I almost forgot to ask you the most important question. What is your new last name going to be? One does need to know her own sister's new married name."

"Honeycutt. I will become Mrs. Stuart Honeycutt. Nice name, don't you agree, *Honey?*"

I laughed. "Your sister's named Honey and you marry a Honeycutt. Yes, a good sign. We'll be Honeycutt and Newberry. You and I will sound like something that's spread on hot English muffins!"

"It could be worse, lady. What if *you* were marrying Stuart? You would be known as Honey Honeycutt."

"Dreadful. Or what if you were Priceless Pearlie Newberry? It's a good thing you're leaving for home, today. I'm being consumed by silliness."

"You are so right, Honey. We each have an advanced case of the giggles."

"One more time, Mary Pearle. I can't resist. Your boobs." I chuckled. "Are they getting *bigger?*"

"No, *longer.*"

We laughed like teenagers. "Longer" would always remain our favorite punch line.

I handed her the first draft of the Creola manuscript to take along. I pointed out the dedication:

This, the story of our beloved nanny, is dedicated to her — Creola Moon — and to Mary Pearle, my big sister and my dearest friend, who shared Creola's magic.

Honored, surprised, and truly moved, my sister burst into tears. No words of gratitude needed to be said. Mary Pearle embraced me. We clung together for an eternity. We cried for what was past and for what was on the horizon. For our sisterhood. For family. For marriages. For four precious children. For deaths, divorce. Books. A wedding. A *new* book. Another wedding. We cried because we were sisters. We cried because we missed our parents and because we missed our Creola. Mostly, we cried because we felt so blessed to have one another.

The next morning, I could hardly say good-bye to Mary Pearle. As my sister drove away, I went inside to tidy up the condo. I tossed my sister's towels and sheets into the washing machine but quickly retrieved them. I wanted to inhale the scent of her perfume one last time. It was sad for me to look where she had posed for a picture. The indentation of her body was still on the living room couch.

I readied myself for a brisk walk. I would attempt to get back into a healthier routine. The downside of her visit had been our total lack of self discipline. We were a terrible influence on one another. We started the week out with good intentions, but soon lapsed into eating too much junk food and allowing exercise to go completely by the wayside. I felt guilty, and she felt fat. But, great goodness above, had it been a wonderful time!

Are your boobs getting bigger? I couldn't laugh again, not just yet.

I walked rapidly — all but ran — toward Beatrice's cottage. I couldn't wait to see my friend. Even with Mary Pearle's company, I'd missed Beatrice and thought about her frequently. Other than at the 'safari' dinner party and chatting a couple of times on the phone, I'd not spent much time with the dear lady, lately.

I wanted to tell her about Mary Pearle's upcoming marriage. I delighted in predicting her reaction. Total surprise? Screams and hugs? Perhaps a cartwheel? It was also possible that Beatrice would be disappointed because there was no longer a need for her as a matchmaker.

I knocked on her door. No answer. I left a note, but there came no response. After several phone calls that day, I left a message on her answering machine. Beatrice abhorred those messages. Predictably, she didn't reply. I didn't worry too terribly much about that, expecting a cheery postcard from her, as before. But none arrived. Where could she be?

Three days later, Oscar called. By then, I was frantic. He said Beatrice was in Atlanta visiting Jennings.

"I was just by the cottage and came upon your note. Poor, dear Beatrice, she's fine, I'm sure. She'd not want to cause you a moment's concern. The dear left rather in a rush. I ran into her quite by happenstance. Beatrice was getting into a cab and shouted to me that Jennings had finally gotten his big break!"

"I'm so relieved to hear she's all right. That's marvelous about Jennings, too."

"I'll say. It's been a long time in coming. Never met the lad myself, but Beatrice has always believed in him, so I do as well."

"Oscar, you've never met her son?"

"No, have you?"

"Not yet, but she and I have been friends

273

for such a short time. I assumed you knew Jennings well."

"I'm afraid not. In some ways, I've known Beatrice for several lifetimes. In other ways, I am no closer to her than are you, my dear."

CHAPTER 15

Soon, Beau and I met Stuart. Both of us genuinely liked the man. In fact, Beau was so taken with him that he offered to host his and Mary Pearle's wedding.

I leapt to my feet when Beau made his generous suggestion. "And we'll have it right here, right here at the beach!"

Mary Pearle didn't know what to say. She'd already made preliminary plans to have a small gathering in her home. Nevertheless, she quickly got into the spirit of the beach venue. She stood up, put her arm around me and, raising her wine glass, roared, "What the heck, I'll just wear my bathing suit. Stuart and I will march right into the Gulf of Mexico!"

"That gets my vote," shouted Stuart.

On a cool September afternoon with a gentle Gulf breeze blowing and the sun about to set, Mary Pearle and Stuart, her daughters, Katy and Susan, Susan's husband Matthew, and Stuart's son, Stuart IV, along with Beau and I and several dear old friends of the bride and of the groom, gathered at the condo. I wanted to invite Beatrice, but she was still visiting Jennings.

In my view, Mary Pearle had never been as peace-filled.

My sister had apparently managed to put her life back together. Even Katy, the daughter who wasn't so sure her mother should remarry, seemed content.

Creola, I know you are smiling down on us this day!

As we sipped pre-wedding champagne, I squeezed Beau's hand and kissed him.

He smiled at me. "What's that for?"

"I'm just glad you and I —"

The sound of a truck cut me off. It pulled into the condo's delivery lot with a rumble we could hear four stories up, through the open balcony doors. "Looks like the caterer has *finally* arrived," Beau groused. "What did you say, Honey?"

"I was saying I'm glad I married you, but looks as if you're more interested in the food."

"No, no, I just —"

"You're just adorable."

I swear, he almost blushed.

A little while later, a minister led our

group to the beach. We gathered at the edge of the tide, in a circle around Mary Pearle and Stuart. As the minister pronounced them man and wife, a wave washed over his feet. Startled, the minister hopped aside — and bumped into Mary Pearle.

Stuart steadied her by one arm. "Wait a minute, sir, this is my wife. I get the first dance!"

Laughter.

The minister recovered. "As I was saying, it is my great pleasure to present Mr. and Mrs. Stuart Honeycutt."

Applause.

Stuart's son embraced Mary Pearle and welcomed her into the Honeycutt family. Her daughters each gave their stepfather a kiss, Susan's with more enthusiasm than Katy's, but hers was a kiss, nonetheless.

Beau said, "Okay folks, let's all go inside and celebrate."

"Wait, wait, we've got to take pictures first!" I quickly gathered the family and friends. As I danced around trying to capture the joy in my sister's face, I noticed her wrinkles had magically melted away. Snap. Snap. My camera popped off shot after shot. The euphoric couple couldn't take their eyes off one another long enough to smile directly into my lens.

"Just look at that sun," I swooned. The brilliant red sunset was picture perfect.

"Can we eat now?" pleaded Beau.

Mary Pearle took her brother-in-law by his arm. "Would somebody please feed this poor, starving man?"

"What the devil is that?" shouted Beau as he broke away from the bride and hurried up the steps toward the condo's swimming pool deck. "Scat, get away, damn bird!" The guests ducked as a pelican soared past them. A large cocktail shrimp fell from the pelican's bill.

I chuckled, "Seems my pelican, like my husband, took too large a bite!"

With the successful wedding behind me, and Beau back in Atlanta, I settled into a final few days of intense editing on the first draft of my book. I ate at my computer, dining on my usual diet of caffeine-rich tea and crackers. So much for my "eat healthier" resolve. I replied only to phone messages from family and from the dearest of friends.

Beatrice called to say she was having the most divine time in Atlanta and that she'd eventually return to her cottage. "We'll have the grandest reunion of all time! That's a promise. Do tell me you forgive me for dashing off in such haste?"

"Of course, Beatrice, I could never be angry with you."

"*Never* is a very strong word, Honey New-berry."

As happy as I was for Mary Pearle, I was sorry that Beatrice hadn't been the person responsible for finding my sister's Prince Charming. She would have relished the challenge.

She agreed. "You do know me well. Naturally, I'm filled with joy for your Mary Pearle. Alas, I did miss a golden opportunity to make a match. I'd tentatively considered Sonny Gilmore. Nice looking. Stable. Certainly well read. A teacher such as your sister would appreciate that quality in a man."

"All good points."

"I thought so. I'd fancied inviting him to your Hawaiian party. Don't you recall, we were going to offer hula lessons? I was to bring my drum!"

"And, we *will* have our luau, just as soon as you get back. So do hurry, please."

"I miss you, and Oscar, our other lovely friends, the birds, *and* my Gulf! Oh dear me, I'm so sea-sick. You must know that is a far more serious condition than is home-sickness!"

"You know the cure."

She ignored my remark. "I do want your Mary Pearle to know how truly happy I am for her and for that gentleman of hers, lucky fellow. I'm certain he is every bit as fine a catch as our bookseller would have been. Honey, you do understand the romantic wanderings of my octogenarian mind? Much of what I say is strictly for fun."

"You're a pip, Beatrice. Please bring yourself back here."

"As soon as I can," she sighed, as her voice trailed away.

"Beatrice, is anything amiss?"

"Definitely *not*. Again, dear girl, I'm sorry. This moment I am on my knees begging you to forgive me for leaving without an appropriate farewell."

"Beatrice, I've been terribly busy myself. Say, wasn't it you who chastised me for saying too many 'I'm sorry's'?"

"Touché! I miss you most dearly, my honey of a friend. Well, tah-tah for now —"

"Don't try to hang up just yet, Beatrice. I'm on pins and needles about Jennings. Do tell me everything about your son's success. Oscar told me the news."

"The announcement will be much better when shared in person. Just as you really wanted to share Mary Pearle's engagement with me. I must run this minute, but, you, young lady, you keep up your good work."

"Wait, wait!"

"I'm off on an adventure, my dear. Beatrice loves you! Tah-tah!"

I slowly put down my phone. How I yearned to sit in Beatrice's cottage and spend precious time with her. Instead, I got back to my computer.

With Mary Pearle away on her honeymoon, my long distance calls were curtailed. So much so that Beau remarked, "What we're saving on phone bills more than pays for the wedding reception."

"You were a dear to give Mary Pearle and Stuart such a generous gift."

"I agree."

E-mails and telephone calls from my editor urged me on. My previous lack of enthusiasm was nothing more than a vague memory. Toward the end of the project, I was e-mailing entire chapters on a twice-daily basis.

One morning on the phone, as we went over a few of the changes in the text, I said, "Honestly, I cannot explain exactly what brought me out of my funk. If I knew, I'd bottle it to sell. Maybe it was being at the beach with so few distractions, or simply the fun I had when my sister and I discussed our memories of Creola. Whatever it was,

Creola's Moonbeam has practically written itself."

What I did not elaborate on was the role Beatrice played. If I'd tried to describe all the essential threads of my transformation, my editor would have fallen asleep. After I hung up, I had to laugh. The answer was simple. Honey Newberry's home remedy for her mid-life crisis had been a spoonful of Creola's heart along with a dash of Beatrice's soul.

As I packed up to return home, Beatrice's absence was my single downer. How I missed seeing that wise and caring woman one more time before I left. However, I could take comfort in knowing my beach-combing buddy was enjoying a long visit with her son.

With the completed manuscript of *Creola's Moonbeam* overnighted to my editor and my bags piled in the car, I locked the condo door and headed north. What a different woman I was from the one who had driven down three months prior. Out of the rearview mirror, I watched as the Gulf faded from view. "See you next summer!"

I'd driven about an hour when I thought about Beau. It was my habit to let him know the moment I was on my way. I called on the cell phone. "It's me, I'll be home for dinner. So, where are you taking me?"

"You mean, after all these weeks of bachelor meals, my woman isn't going to cook my supper?"

"You're a much better cook than me. Tell you what, I'll pick up something for us. How about Mexican?"

"I'm teasing you, Honey. We are going out. I have something to tell you."

"An announcement in a public place. Uh oh, you must have bad news. A different woman in your life?"

"Worse."

"What do you mean 'worse'? Is it Mary Catherine? Butlar? Beau, what is it?"

"I'm sorry, Honey, it's not a bad thing. In fact, this is something good, and, I believe, exciting."

"A puppy? Oh Beau, I'm just not ready, not yet. Nestle's not been gone long enough. You know I'm still grieving."

"Wrong, again. Stop trying to guess. Honey, the surprise is that I've found a new house. Can't wait for you to see it!"

I nearly ran off the road. I could hardly form words, but finally uttered, "We're moving? A new home?"

"Well, it's actually an old one, but it's the best kind of old. The historical kind. Honey, it's over one hundred years old! Once we've fixed it up, we will really have something."

Each and every one of our disastrous house projects flashed before me like a dying man's life passes before him when he stands on the gallows. "You can't be serious." I all but *spit* as I laundry-listed every renovation mishap in our twenty-plus-year ordeal. "Beloved husband, do you not remember saying, 'A little wallpaper, a bit of paint, we'll have a palace.' It took two long, horrible decades to make that statement a reality!"

"Exactly. Now we know what we're doing. It'll be fun."

Our connection crackled and faded. Either my cell phone cut out or the Lord Himself ended our conversation. I pulled into a service station and purchased a large Coke and giant-sized box of crackers. The entire box was gone by the time I passed a "Welcome to Georgia" sign on the interstate. I called Beau at his office, only to discover he was at lunch.

I grew more apprehensive with each mile. The house in question must be something special, because Beau Newberry was *not* the moving type. Could my husband actually be in the early stages of dementia?

Having time to think about the situation,

I questioned myself. Had I not always hated our ranch house? Was I not the very same woman, who, for years, dreamed of moving?

Twice, we almost had.

REAL ESTATE

BY HONEY NEWBERRY

I found out beyond a shadow of a doubt that my husband loved me. One Friday came a phone call from my friend, Knoxie. She was a brand-new real estate agent.

"Honey, you won't believe it. There's a lady in my neighborhood who wants to buy your house. She's says she's crazy about it!"

"I bet you're right about the 'she's crazy' part."

In truth, I was flattered that someone appreciated our home. Beau and I had worked mighty hard to improve it. I was all the more interested when Knoxie mentioned how much the woman was willing to pay.

"You have my attention, now."

"Tell you what, Honey. Are you busy today?"

"Nothing that can't wait. The children are in school, why?"

"Get ready, I'm coming to pick you up. We'll take a look at some houses. I already have three in mind. How about it?"

This opportunity was not to be ignored. Twenty minutes later, we were in Knoxie's car, going over her list of possibilities.

By that afternoon, we'd found "the" house. Newer than ours, it had a nice floor plan, was closer to the children's schools, and also had a lovely updated kitchen. Ours still sported late 50's pink appliances and a dark-red linoleum floor. I was ready to sign the papers.

My poor, unsuspecting Beau drove into our garage. The man was ready for a nice, quiet weekend and had not a clue he was about to be broadsided. What Beau had in mind was a relaxed round of golf on Saturday followed by a movie that night. (That's movie, not *move*). I met him as he stepped from his car. He was startled. I was all but frothing at the mouth.

Knoxie was positioned safely behind me.

"Guess what? We're selling our house! That's not all, either. I've found a new one!"

Beau stumbled backwards into his car. Gripping the steering wheel, his knuckles white, my husband gritted his teeth and took a deep breath. As if the man hadn't heard me correctly, I repeated my news, "I said someone wants to buy our house. Even better, there's another one we can buy *to-day!*"

This was the moment my longsuffering husband genuinely proved his love for me. After driving home bumper to bumper in Atlanta's legendary five o'clock traffic, Beau got back into that traffic just please me. Visions of his golf game, popcorn, and a movie burst like a billion tiny bubbles.

When we got to the new house, we parked by the *For Sale* sign.

"Hmm, it seems smaller than before," I noted. "The yard sure needs work."

We went inside. Nice living room, spacious dining room. Down the hall we headed with me in the lead followed by a somewhat skeptical Beau. Knoxie, third-in-line and still encouraged, was holding a more neutral position in order to give the two of us our space.

Besides the master suite, which I coveted, the children's rooms didn't compare in size to what Mary Catherine and Butlar presently enjoyed. When I admitted that point, Beau's face brightened. The kitchen wasn't quite as magnificent as it appeared on first impression.

All and all, I no longer adored the house.

Beau uttered an audible sigh of relief.

Maybe I got cold feet because it happened

too quickly. But for whatever reason, we neither bought nor sold a house that Friday. I thanked Knoxie for her time. Beau smiled affably, played golf on Saturday, and took me out for dinner and to see a romantic movie. The popcorn was very fresh, and so was my husband.

Our second potential change of address came about a couple of years later. That time around, we decided to work with a builder. We selected plans for an L-shaped home which would be built in a new subdivision in our neighborhood, one right around the corner. The builder even agreed to add a picket fence in front. My lifelong ambition has been to have a home with a white picket fence.

All we had to do was sell our current house.

I again contacted Knoxie, who arranged for a caravan of real estate agents to come by the next Tuesday. Their cars pulled into our driveway. Doors slammed and agents invaded. Ten or twelve of them trooped about, inspecting, making notes, and talking a strange buyer-seller language among themselves.

I felt as if I were inside a fort under fire.

"How many walls have you folks knocked out?"

Nervously, I responded. "Not too many, I suppose. You'll notice the house remains standing." No one laughed. "Hmmm. Well, I've never actually counted, let's see. Initially, just the one wall in the family room. That is, if you don't count the sliding glass doors as walls. If you do, that would be three, in total."

Someone scribbled on a yellow legal pad.

I well-remembered the night Beau and I knocked out the wall which separated the kitchen from the family room. It was a spontaneous project, a way to distract us from our worries. During dinner we'd been glued to the TV watching coverage of Desert Storm. This was the first fierce nighttime attack on Baghdad. Beau and I were very worried about our two nephews — his sister's sons — both of whom were talking about joining the army. The young men, college students, were just the right ages to go to Iraq.

We moved the couch away from the wall and started to bash out door frames and paneling.

The Patriot missiles were launched.

Beau kicked out sheetrock.

The evening sky of Baghdad was bright with ominous blasts of fire. Bombs exploded.

I swept up rubble.

Desert Storm ended in just a few days. The boys remained in college. We could walk directly from the kitchen into the family room.

"Oh, wait." The agents began to grow impatient.

I tapped my head as I mentioned something else. "There was also the big supporting wall we took out to enlarge the master bedroom. Also, do you think an outside wall should count since it's now a bay window?"

The agents stared at me.

"So," interjected Knoxie, "Honey is trying to tell you seven or eight walls have been removed to create better flow."

"Yes, that's it, flow." I nodded like a wooden puppet. As if my strings were being manipulated, I continued, "If you'll notice, we *do* have excellent flow."

My friend, Betty Ann, once commented that every time she visits, she finds another wall missing. "I worry that one day I'll come, and your whole home will have caved in like a house of cards!"

The realtors seemed to be having the same thought. I changed the subject. Leading them onward, I pointed out the mantel downstairs, one that we'd purchased at the Scott's Antiques Show in south Atlanta, and hauled home on the roof of our old station wagon. Beau had worked diligently to refinish the piece. His efforts had paid off; it's a beauty.

"Wonderful mantel," said Knoxie.

An agent nodded, "Of course, that will stay."

Stay? After all the effort Beau put into it? She couldn't be serious, could she? Leaving that mantle would be like abandoning a much-loved puppy to an unappreciative stranger. I was beginning to make mental notes of my own.

When I led the caravan outside, the realtors jotted down "brick walkways."

"My husband built them."

"There's another lovely walk around on the other side of the house," Knoxie added.

"That's right, when we had the sunroom built in 1983, the workmen ripped out the original screen porch and pitched all the bricks into the middle of the yard. My husband carefully cleaned the cement from each and every brick and used them to lay his walks. He suffered painful cuts and bruises on his hands and on his arms and knees."

The realtors only grunted.

I looked around the yard while the agents checked out the swimming pool. My eyes went to the initials carved on the patio's concrete. "HN + BN." An agent toed it with the tip of her shoe. "This can be removed," she told the others.

I thought about Butlar's childhood scribbling on the basement stairway wall. When he was in second grade, our little boy had painted in block letters, "I love this house." I'd left the inscription in place. No doubt, if I escorted the agents down there, one of them would bleat, "This can be removed."

My eyes filled with tears. *Mom loves this house, too.*

That was the end of the new home with the picket fence. I took Knoxie to lunch and apologized for once again wasting her time. Not too long afterwards, Knoxie went into teaching.

CHAPTER 16

I pulled into the driveway and pushed the button to raise the garage door. Up it went. That it still worked was a novelty. Throughout the years, the door had suffered frequent abuse from "Butts Up," a rowdy game our children played with tennis balls. Later on, it was habitually thrown off its track by not-so-gentle wallops as the kids learned to drive at the wheel of my station wagon. And, as recently as the previous springtime, we'd chosen to leave the door up for an entire month, to provide a safe ledge for a nest of baby wrens.

I rushed indoors and found Beau. "Howdy, stranger."

He hugged and kissed me. "I missed you, lady."

"I missed you, too. Even though you visited a couple of times, a whole summer away is too long for this gal."

"And for her man." Beau stepped back. "I

can't do it, Honey."

"Can't do what?"

"While I was waiting for you to get here, I went over to the new house. It's in the historic district and has those high ceilings you've always wanted and those porches all around. It's a great house. But, I, I can't leave this one."

I smiled. "I know, Beau, just look around, these walls tell our family's story. Or, perhaps, it's actually the *lack* of walls that says so much about us."

"I'm surprised the whole damn thing never collapsed."

"I guess we got lucky." I hugged him again. "Tell you what, Beau, do you want me to go and see the house with you? I don't want us to miss out on a potential dream home."

"Honey, we're standing in my dream home."

"I agree." In truth, given my rather impetuous nature, I really didn't want to put myself in temptation's way. "So, Mr. Newberry, what do you say that we go out and get some dinner?"

"That won't be necessary." Beau walked me out onto the deck. I smelled his feast cooking on the grill.

"Yum!"

"Welcome home, Honey."

I took a long, lingering look at the back-yard. "I'm so glad to be home. Why, I hardly miss the Gulf."

"It must be my cooking!"

It felt fantastic to be getting back into the limelight. The publisher scheduled the release of *Creola's Moonbeam* the next spring, just in time for one of my favorite book festivals. The event was one where I was sure to come across many fellow authors, some of whom were close friends.

I immediately ran into the charming Southern gentleman, J. Kershaw Cooper, whose short stories made him the toast of his proud South Georgia town. I found Jerry Lee Davis standing next to his table, where, as usual, he was talking to people. There's always a crowd around Jerry Lee. A talented and genial young man, he had written a number of successful projects, including a novel, two plays and a documentary film.

I was delighted to meet up with my dear friend, Jacklyn White, who for months had e-mailed and telephoned with gentle but firm suggestions to get busy. A retired police officer and multitalented author, Jackie writes true-crime books — perfectly researched stories about famous and infamous Georgians — and most recently had embarked on fiction. She does everything well.

This feels like a homecoming, I told myself, as I slowly made way to my booth. I wondered why it had taken me so long to get back into the swing of things. *It's just the way you are. Don't beat yourself up; enjoy the moment.* I sounded like an affirmation tape.

As abundantly thankful as I was for the three months at the Gulf, for visits from Beau, the children, and Mary Pearle, and for her beach wedding, I was equally jubilant that the vacation had birthed my book. Well, best make that "our" book, since Mary Pearle would surely correct me about that oversight. My sister remained appreciative and overwhelmed by the credit I'd given for her input into *Creola's Moonbeam.* Mary Pearle had become the toast of her town — Birmingham, Alabama — with her new husband Stuart on one arm and our book on the other.

How proud you must be, Creola, of us, your girls, Mary Pearle and me.

My thoughts then turned to Beatrice. Friendship with the charismatic woman was the dessert of my summer's memories.

Rounding a corner, I spotted a familiar face in a booth to my left. It couldn't be.

Could it?

"Beatrice!"

"Hello, there!"

She was seated behind a booth table. I rushed to her side, bent down, and threw my arms around her. "What on earth are you doing here?"

"You have only yourself to blame."

"I can't imagine what you are talking about. But for whatever reason, I'm beyond happy to see you! How did you know I'd be at the festival today?"

"An old bird like me knows more than you'd think. I always had faith in your Creola Moon and even more so in her Moonbeam. Actually, I was more surprised to find *myself* here."

"Do I hear humility creeping in? We must exhibit more confidence in ourselves, young lady!" I mimicked gently.

"Yes ma'am," Beatrice replied primly. She pointed to a chair beside her. "You'd best have a seat, young lady. I have something to show you."

Curious, I obeyed. Out of the corner of my eye, I saw some books stacked on the table's end, but paid no real attention. It was on Beatrice I focused.

Speaking as if a teacher to her student, Beatrice cleared her throat and began, "Of course, you remember how I badgered you to publish not just your stories about Creola, but your stories about your own life?"

"How could I forget?"

"But, dear heart, you'd given up. 'Use them to fire up your barbecue,' said you."

"Guilty."

Beatrice pursed her lips and fluttered her eyelashes. "I simply took the bull by the horns, as my former husband, ah yes, as Carlos used to say. Take a look at *this*."

Beatrice took a book from the top of the stack and presented me with it. The bright yellow cover framed a pretty watercolor painting of a suburban ranch house. Its front yard was filled with a flock of pink plastic flamingos surrounding a family of four. The author's name was concealed by a sticker reading *Autographed Copy*. But the title left no doubt what this book was. *Honey's Beeswax*.

I looked at Beatrice. "I'm simply thunderstruck! *Honey's Beeswax*. I don't know what to say." I shook my head and frowned. "Beatrice, you never *would* admit you're a writer. You've blown your cover now!"

"I'm *not* a writer. I merely made a few mental notes about the crazy things you told me as we walked on the beach. Then, after I read the stories you sent me on the computer disc, I merely added some organization and some artwork."

"*Merely?* I'm speechless."

"Thank goodness you weren't speechless last summer, or we'd not be sitting here today."

"You make a valid point."

"Look inside, see my drawings? You are permitted to give me a great deal of acclaim for these!"

"Oh my goodness, yes, I certainly will!"

"Yes, indeed. There's the scene with the bomb squad and your son's hand grenade."

"How I love the look on the neighbor's face! That's Bruce, perfectly!"

"And surely you remember the raccoon in your attic?"

"Wish I *could* forget. That poor, frightened creature! His hair is standing on end."

I thumbed through the beautifully detailed pen-and-ink drawings accompanying each chapter. As I'd suspected during my very first visit to her cottage, drawing was Beatrice's forte. "Your artwork is amazing."

"Of course, it is."

"Author, artist, and you're modest, as well."

"One can't be too humble." Beatrice pointed to the story about Beau and I getting locked in the cemetery. "That's one of my favorites."

"I love the expression you drew for Beau when the bolt cutters broke."

"Captured his shock, I thought."

"He'll appreciate that."

I turned to the chapter about the roof work. "I can almost feel rain on my face."

"Honey, I'm so glad you are pleased. Just remember, you did all the telling, dear girl. I simply put it down on paper. It took me about three weeks, perhaps four. No, I must be completely honest with you. The compilation, I'll not call it 'writing,' was a good five weeks of off-and-on work. I did take time to do other things, but only to avoid making you feel too guilty. I know how you are."

"You *do* know me well."

"I added a few sketches and made a phone call to an old friend who owns a printing company."

"A former husband?"

"Heavens no, not even a boyfriend. But, Honey, don't you see? Your personal stories are now, finally, a book."

"With more than a little help from you. Thank you, my friend."

Was I surprised? Definitely.

Embarrassed? Some.

Angry? Maybe a little. I was angry with

myself for not sticking to the task of completing my own work. I thought back to the morning when I pitched all the stories in the garbage.

But no, anger wasn't exactly what I was feeling either. In truth, it was gratitude. Beatrice had accomplished something that I couldn't or simply *didn't* do for myself. I was feeling sincerely grateful for her perseverance.

"I was right on one point, my talented friend. You are a terrific artist."

"Merely a hobby, mine are only doodles, my dear."

"Will you look at this one!"

Several years prior, Beau had had it with a cottonwood tree that sprouted into a real Jack in the Beanstalk tree. The gargantuan plant seemed to grow two feet every time Beau turned his back on it. Within a few years, the cottonwood towered over our house, stretching its limbs over half the roof. The wicked tree produced round, nut-like fruits which it rained down on our driveway. We took our lives in our hands every time we carried out the garbage. It was like navigating a field of greased marbles.

Armed with his chainsaw, Beau climbed atop our roof and attacked. "Tree, you are *mine*."

There was something strikingly fiendish about my husband's intensity. One by one, branches dropped to the ground. The man was in his glory, but the tree fought for one last victory. It conjured up a curse. Beau had cut all but the last three limbs when suddenly he started to slip. Only a strong gutter kept him from a serious injury. Because he didn't get hurt, the scene in my story was very, very funny. So was Beatrice's sketch of it.

"Beatrice, you really captured Beau's panic. Look at the stark terror in his eyes! I love how you drew the ends of his fingernails flying off as he's desperately trying to grip roof shingles."

Thanks to Beau's new fear of heights, the tree, which had assumed a palm-like shape, was eventually taken down by a professional. It became kindling which, try as we did, would never burn.

In that way, I suppose, the tree did triumph.

"And look at this sketch! Thank you, Beatrice, for making me appear rather fetching in this drawing with the kitchen mop. Why, you made me almost svelte. I still can't believe my inventive and *usually* successful husband actually attempted to unclog the sink using the garden hose."

Beatrice laughed. "Get towels, lots of towels," she said in a deep voice, mimicking Beau. "I've broken the whole damn house!"

"What a disaster. Though it wasn't a laughing matter that night. It was almost eleven o'clock before Beau gave in and called a plumber. The only one we could find at that late hour rolled in, literally *rolled* in, around midnight. Weaving and bobbing like a buoy, the aged hippy was as drunk as a skunk."

"Speaking of skunks." Beatrice flipped pages to one of the last chapters. "I included the ill-fated creature who got himself lodged in your heat vent. I'd never before drawn a skunk's eyes! Took me a few tries to capture his glower. I eventually turned back to one of my sketches of Beau for inspiration."

We both laughed.

She added, "Who would think that shooting the skunk with a tranquilizer gun would cause him to spray?"

"Apparently it was news to our exterminator, too."

"Did it really cost four-hundred dollars to get rid of the stench?"

"Yes, and it was worth every cent."

"Don't you mean 'scent'? Excuse the pun, ah-hem."

I happily skimmed through the other

sketches. "I was curious about how you captured our faces so well. Especially Beau."

"I knew your facial structure well enough to draw you from memory, but Beau wasn't as familiar to me. Remember the night Beau cooked the steaks for us? When you were busy in the kitchen and he was cooking at the grill, I made some preliminary sketches of his features. It was as easy as pie to adjust his wonderfully expressive face for the drawings."

"This book has been your plan for some time, I see."

"Yes, of course."

"I can't wait to show it to my family."

Beatrice handed me a copy tied up with ribbon and bow. A rolled sheet of artist's paper was tucked inside the bow. "A small token from me to thee. Open the book, Honey, there's an inscription inside."

I unfurled the paper. It was Beatrice's drawing of Beau and me standing on the beach with the Gulf of Mexico in the background.

I beamed. "This is a treasure, truly it is. Thank you!"

"You're welcome."

I opened the book.

My dear Honey,

This IS your book. I just put a few appropriate sketches in with your well-scripted words. You will never know how much our strolls on the beach meant to me. Thank you for your stories, thank you for your time, and most of all, thank you for your friendship.

I rejoice that you are counted among my Dear Ones.

Sincerely, Beatrice

I was in tears. I clutched the book to my chest and leaned over to give my friend another hug. Then, out of the corner of my eye, I spotted it. A brilliantly colored, hand-painted shawl was draped around a wheel-chair, one folded up and put to the side behind a box of books. Hers. It had to be. The shawl suddenly slid to the floor to reveal Beatrice's secret.

I was speechless.

Beatrice smiled. "Uh oh, I see you've noticed my new mode of transportation."

I nodded.

"I've had to use it more and more of late. The truth is, I have to use the blasted thing all the time. Last summer was fantastic for me because I could walk for a couple of hours, sometimes longer, each day. Often my spurts of energy arose from the joy you brought to me."

"Only two hours?"

"Yes, sadly, my illness does limit me."

"You gave me your *only* walking time?"

"Don't be so dramatic, my dear. Those magical hours made up the best minutes of my days. And, don't you dare forget, the pleasure of your company added many hours for me."

"Oh, Beatrice."

"Now, don't you start!" Her English accent theatrically enhanced, it became apparent that the fiercely proud woman wanted no sympathy from me. "In actual fact, I can get along much more efficiently using my chair. Why, I'm faster than I've been in years."

A voice came over the loudspeaker. "Attention, authors, please get to your places, your customers will be entering the building in ten minutes."

"You need to go to your own booth, now," Beatrice said gently.

I refused to leave. I needed to be with Beatrice, to simply "be." She understood. I continued to gaze at her and, sadly, at the wheelchair which now held her frail form captive. Beatrice ignored any sympathy I offered. She was uncomfortable with any show of pity.

In a few minutes, a couple came up and thumbed through "*Honey's Beeswax*." Beatrice seemed relieved by the diversion. "Excuse me, Honey, while I sign my work. Paying customers, you do understand."

I feigned being miffed. I needed time to compose myself.

The couple purchased several copies as gifts. "We could share some funny experiences about living in an older home," the wife said. "George and I surely will recognize one another in these pages!"

The husband commented, "Judging from the drawings, your hero sounds like as big a bozo as me!"

Beatrice defended Beau, "Oh yes, but as of late, our hero has become quite capable."

When the couple moved on, I said, "How can you keep a straight face with me sitting here? This is so bizarre. Didn't you want to say, 'Look, there stands Mrs. Bozo'?"

"I am very much an actress, didn't you know?"

"Is there no end to your secrets?"

"I was a bit concerned that you'd be angry with me. After all, I did filch your work."

"Beatrice, I meant it when I suggested that you use these stories as you please. All they were doing was sitting in my computer for me to read from time to time. You've given the characters life. Not only that, you've added your marvelous drawings. I just wish I'd thought about artwork, myself. Your sketches truly enhance the words. By the way, will you please tell the cover artist how well I thought that turned out? I love the pink flamingoes!" I'd written a story about Beau's office buddies surprising us with the plastic flock as a prank.

Beatrice patted herself on the back. "Thank you so much, you very fine water-colorist, you!"

I stared at her tearfully, again. "You do it all, my friend, you do it all."

Beatrice accepted my praise with a smug sigh.

"Now, to business. I want to buy copies for my friends, that is, if you will kindly favor me with autographs."

"My pleasure."

"I'll take ten books, please. You will accept a personal check?"

"If you'll produce proper identification, stranger. Silly woman, of course, I will!" Beatrice pantomimed ringing a bell. "You're sure to be my big sale of the day, Honey Newberry!"

While Beatrice was signing the copies, I wrote a check and asked her about Jennings.

Beatrice replied, "He's smashing, darling

girl, he's simply smashing. You and I will do lunch one day soon, and I will fill you in on everything my fabulous young man is doing."

"I'd enjoy that. But, please include your son. I can't wait much longer to meet him."

Another customer walked up and Beatrice turned her attention to the woman. "I've kept you here far too long, Honey. It's really very sweet of you to stay, but from one author to another, I must insist that you go and man your own table."

"That can wait. Besides, I can watch my place from here. Look, Beatrice, you can see my publicist, the lady wearing the green and white suit, she's sitting there with *Creola's Moonbeam*. Also, I've got my cell phone and she can quickly signal me."

"Whatever you say, dear."

"I've missed you. I'm overjoyed to find you here!"

"I planned it."

"I don't doubt that one iota."

"Deary me, don't let me forget. I must, simply *must* purchase my own copy of *Creola's Moonbeam*. It will be signed, naturally?"

I produced one from my bag. "Happened to have a copy with me, and it's yours. No charge."

"What? A freebee? Marvelous! Thank you."

With that I quickly penned a few words:

My dear Beatrice,

Creola's Moonbeam would never have come to be without your influence and support. Thank you for that remarkable gift, in truth, for the gift of yourself. That said, your counting me among your Dear Ones is your greatest gift of all.

I hope you will enjoy reading about Creola with the understanding that you took up where she left off.

With my love, Honey

"Thank you," Beatrice said. My throat was too tight to answer. I just nodded. Beatrice went on, "I've been very pleased with the interest in this book. People really like your stories, Honey. Those who have read *Honey's Beeswax* tell me that they identify with your experiences."

"That's nice. Beatrice, let's not talk about the book. Let's talk about you. I want to know —"

"Now, now. I'd rather discuss the book." Beatrice then sat ramrod straight, looked at me for a moment, then said quietly, "My dear Honey of a friend, I suspect it will sell all of its first printing well before I die."

I put my face into my hands and cried.

"Not don't you get maudlin on me, Mrs. Newberry." Beatrice gently touched my shoulder. "Just look at it from my point of view. I'll get to do cartwheels in Heaven."

I sat there, crying, and laughing.

Creola whispered in my ear. *Life's all about how we live, Moonbeam. Not how we die.*

CHAPTER 17

I dressed slowly for Beatrice's memorial service. Beau offered to drive me, but I insisted on going alone.

The ceremony, held in Atlanta, was extremely well-attended, especially considering Beatrice hadn't lived in the city for years. "Lived." It was devastating for me to realize that Beatrice no longer *lived.*

Everyone was saying much the same thing. The charismatic woman was the type of person who was never expected to die. To her Dear Ones, like me, Beatrice seemed immortal.

I had the immediate consolation of seeing people about whom she had so frequently talked. I was meeting my fellow Dear Ones, the remarkable artists and writers who peopled Beatrice's world. I was surprised and honored to learn that many of them had actually heard of me.

As I perused the crowd, the artists were

particularly easy to spot. I made that assessment based mostly on their garb — flowing fabrics, hats with flowers and feathers, and fabulous jewelry, likely hand-crafted, one-of-a-kind pieces, many with the flavor of international travel. There was very little in the style of a typical Southern mourning. The church was awash with reds and oranges, bright pinks and yellows.

My own somber outfit was embarrassingly out of place. Even so, my blue dress had been carefully selected. It was the soft slate of a Blue Heron, the blue of a Gulf coast sky just before a summer storm. My thought was to bring her much-loved Gulf of Mexico to Beatrice for one last time.

"Honey!"

In his kilt with all the trimmings, Oscar broke through a group of people and gave me a warm and sincere embrace. It was if I was being hugged by a small bear. I appreciated every squeeze from the burly little gray-haired beast.

"Oscar, dear man. I'm very, very sorry. Are you holding up all right?"

"My heart is broken."

"You two had been friends for so long, I know."

"Beatrice was my wife."

"Wife!"

"Aye."

"But she said —"

"Oh, she did like her little jokes."

I felt as if I might faint on the spot. Wife. Husband. Mary Pearle had been right when she suggested there was more to Oscar and Beatrice's relationship.

"Aye, my wife, that she was, the dear darling. I can no longer remember which years we were married, nor between which two husbands I fit. I like to believe I was one of her favorites."

I hugged Oscar once again. "Oscar, she once told me that you were the 'Dearest of her Dear Ones.' You are absolutely right to think she was partial to her handsome Scot."

"There you have it, girl! I was the *only* Scot, as well!"

An Indian woman in a sari walked up and put her arm around Oscar.

He politely introduced me, then I sent him on his way. "You must go ahead, 'Dearest One,' you have many guests to greet."

"I shall return to talk with you again, dear Honey. I promise you that." With those words, Oscar was swept into a sea of Beatrice's friends.

The ceremony began amidst glorious music — exotic chants and quirky rhythms, a bit of opera, a bit of whimsical folk music.

Beatrice would have delighted in the choir's choices. Wait, silly woman, what was I thinking? Beatrice most assuredly orchestrated the service herself. A smile curled my lips.

Next, people rose one-by-one to share marvelous "Miss Bea" stories.

The traveling friends talked of journeys abroad with her, trips to China, to Australia, to Hawaii, and to her native England. There were tales of cruises, of raft trips, and of hot air balloon rides, of traveling on the Orient Express, and of boarding a camel on the occasion of our dearly departed's seventy-fifth birthday.

Her artist buddies spun yarns about work, exhibitions, triumphs, and about Beatrice's sincere passion to encourage others.

A handsome young man, one she had mentored, lamented, "Had Miss Bea not been so intent on helping all of us, she could have been better known for her own art and writing throughout the whole country. No, around the world. No! Miss Bea could have been a *galactic* success! But this grand woman, one whom we all adored, was singular in concern for those coming after her."

Every person in the church seated suddenly rose to his feet and burst into a

spontaneous round of raucous applause. The walls of the old building shook from the thunder of our collective gratitude.

An attractive woman in a bright-orange suit stood next. "Our family had its own Auntie Mame," she said. "First of all, I must explain my outfit. When Aunt Beattie finally admitted her end was near, she made me promise to wear her favorite color. Bright orange. I argued, of course, but whoever won an argument with this woman?"

The congregation, again seated, clapped in agreement.

"In this sea of brilliant color, I actually appear rather drab. Apparently our aunt discussed what to wear with many among you. Let's just agree, as always, our Beatrice has made her point!"

I looked down at my staid blue suit and wished I'd worn orange, too.

Oscar took to the podium. So overcome was he that he could not speak his well-prepared text. He disappeared for a moment, then returned carrying Beatrice's drum. Slowly he pounded out a few pained sounds that seemed to match the sorrow of his own heartbeat. Afterwards, silence choked the congregation. A woman helped Oscar to his seat.

One by one, tribute after tribute, each

person shared something else that touched my soul. Even in her death, Beatrice exuded wonderment. But I found myself searching the room for the person Beatrice surely wanted to hear from most. Where was Jennings? Maybe, like Oscar, he was too grief-stricken to speak.

At the conclusion of the service, I gathered my courage and approached the niece, the lady in orange.

"Excuse me, please. I know you need to talk with many people, but, just briefly, my name is Honey Newberry and . . ."

"Yes, of course! I'm Cynthia. Certainly I know who you are, Mrs. Newberry. Or if I may, Honey?"

"Honey, please."

"You are my aunt's friend from the beach, the author. It was your stories that kept our darling Aunt Beattie going for many more months than the doctors had allotted her. It is I who should thank you, Honey."

"I don't deserve your compliments, Cynthia. I did nothing. It was Beatrice who did so much for me."

Sounding like her aunt, the young woman begged to differ. "Let's just call it a draw!"

"Cynthia, may I ask you one quick question?" Responding to her affirmative nod, I continued, "Where will I find Jennings?"

"Who?"

"Her son, your cousin Jennings."

"I'm, I'm sorry, I'm afraid I must tell you there is no Jennings. Aunt Beattie never had children."

My mouth dropped open.

"My poor dear Honey, I'm afraid you were a partner to one of our Beatrice's many charms. When my aunt wished hard enough for something, it became a reality for her."

I stood there silently. Shaking.

"On the other hand, more often than not, her whims became reality for the rest of us, too," Cynthia continued. "Such was the case with her art, with her adventures around the world, with her chosen friendships, with her Dear Ones, and with us, those fortunate enough to be members of her family. Honey, your book was just that, a dream she made come true. Beatrice willed it and it was so!"

"I just don't know what to say. Jennings was a real person to me!"

Cynthia smiled. "Let him remain real to you. You know something? In an odd way, Honey, you may have replaced Aunt Beattie's fictional son, in her mind, at least."

"What?"

"Yes, toward the end, Aunt Beattie became a bit befuddled. From time to time, she'd talk to 'my little girl, Honey' or on occasion, there was another name. Let's see. Oh, yes, she'd say, 'Don't be so self deprecating, Harriette!' I figured Harriette and Honey could be one and the same? Yes?"

"Yes. Your aunt worked hard to exorcise Miss Harriette from me. It's a long story."

"I'd like to hear that story. Perhaps we can spend some time together?"

"That would be nice."

I embraced the niece, thanked her, and promised that we would make plans to visit when she was ready. Dazed, I wandered out and got into my car.

At the festival, I'd stuffed my autographed copy of *Honey's Beeswax* into a tote bag. The bag had remained in the corner of my study ever since. I knew exactly where it was, too. I'd looked at it every single time I went into the room. Each time, the book called to me. Each time I chose to ignore its plea for attention.

Why was I so reluctant to open the book Beatrice had lovingly created from my stories? Was this a testament to my own shortcomings? Given the discovery of my friend's terminal illness, was it simply too painful for me to look at her artwork? My face reddened. Guilt swept over me like an ice cold wave.

As I drove along the expressway, I began beating myself up for not visiting Beatrice before she died. Creola's face came into my mind. I hadn't visited my darling Crellie often enough, either.

"Honey Newberry, you are so damned self-involved. Will you ever learn? You don't deserve to be a called a 'honey of a friend.' Can you hear me, Beatrice? I am sincerely sorry. I'm sorry I didn't visit you. I'm abundantly sorry that I can't bring myself to look at the book you made for me." Tears flooded my face. I could hardly see to drive.

I pulled into a rest stop and sat there talking out loud some more. "I merely thumbed through your book, your drawings, your work; then simply ignored your fine accomplishment. How negligent I was! Forgive me, please, forgive me, my dear, dear friend."

I buried my head in my arms. Resting on the steering wheel, I sobbed, "I'm sorry." Reaching for a tissue, I wiped my eyes and blew my nose. "I am so sorry. I'm even sorry that I'm sorry!"

You sure do enjoy having an attack of 'the sorry's,' Creola whispered.

Indeed, Beatrice added. *Dear girl, get over it.*

I started to smile.

"All right, Beatrice. All right, Crellie." I started my car and pulled back onto the highway. I vowed to myself that I would look at every page of *Honey's Beeswax*. How I longed to relive the day of the book festival, the day Beatrice penned her dear message to me. The last day I was to see the extraordinary lady alive.

Beau wasn't home when I pulled in the garage. Walking inside, I put on some soothing music, prepared a cup of tea, took off my heels, and curled up into my soft, comfy chair.

At Beatrice's suggestion, I'd purchased the chair soon after returning from the beach. Even an ordinary chair now held special meaning for me. I sipped the tea as I munched on an English muffin. The muffin was fitting, in Beatrice's honor. I spread on fig preserves, a favorite of Creola's, and another appropriate choice for a day to be bathed in memory. Everything perfect, I opened *Honey's Beeswax* and began to read the stories I had tried to throw away but Beatrice had rescued, just as she'd rescued me.

Around me, my house came to life. I could see the stories unfolding as they occurred, in the kitchen and the family room and dining room. How well I remembered knocking out the pantry wall only to say, "Now what do we do, Beau?" Another *whoops* in the making?

All those now-gone walls: the one between the kitchen and the den that Beau took down as war broke out, those walls appeared and disappeared with the blink of an eye as I reread my stories. Wallpapers, three different ones in the kitchen; paint colors, as many as six in the den, I could swap about in the pages on my lap.

I laughed with gusto as I again envisioned Butlar's legs dangling from the attic floor through the kitchen ceiling. Thankfully unharmed was our nine-year-old boy, unhurt but for his bruised ego, as he enthusiastically tried to help his Daddy with the new insulation. Yet another example of an incident that was "funny after the fact."

The plastic, pink flamingo flock we'd once endured in the front yard, and white automobile tires filled with dead plants — both moving-in pranks from Beau's office buddies — were once again there in the front yard, just as they appeared on the cover of Beatrice's book.

I turned around and looked out a window at the swimming pool which had been the longest ordeal and greatest fiasco of all. It made up an entire chapter in the book. We'd begun building it one spring, but our usual bad luck interfered to keep construction going through the entire summer. The pool wasn't finished and filled with water until Halloween. Undaunted, our two children and every one of their neighborhood friends decided to inaugurate it.

Wearing Halloween costumes, the squealing kids pinched their noses and cannonballed into our brand new pool. Our soggy Spiderman and Wicked Witch, along with an assortment of other equally well-saturated monsters, vampires, and hobgoblins, climbed out of the water into awaiting beach towels. If not for the intervention of their parents, the cold, soggy Trick-or-Treaters would have hit the neighborhood for Halloween goodies. Of course, many had to go as ghosts — wearing sheets — because there was not time enough to dry their costumes!

"Mom, this is soooo cool," shouted Butlar as he scurried out the door in his quickly contrived hunchback (pillow and buckskin shirt) outfit. "We get to go swimming *and* Trick or Treating, all on the same day!"

It was nothing short of a miracle that no one had caught pneumonia. But then, happy miracles do occur.

I hugged the book to my chest, then

opened it again to read more stories. For the first time, I noticed the title page just inside the cover.

Honey's Beeswax
by Harriette Ophelia Butlar Newberry

What had I seen?
"By Harriette Ophelia Butlar Newberry."
I quickly checked the cover, peeling back the *Autographed Copy* sticker. Sure enough, hidden underneath was my full name. Not Honey Newberry, as on my other books, but Harriette Ophelia Butlar Newberry, an altogether different person!

As if on cue, the doorbell rang. There stood the postman.

"Sign here, ma'am." He handed me a registered letter. I opened it.

Dear Honey,
You know all too well my beloved aunt, so you understand that you now have an important assignment. Aunt Beatrice and I wish you the best of luck in selling your newest book. She insists you have your publisher print thousands more copies.

I'll look forward to a glowing report

from you at a future luncheon meeting.

Sincerely, Cynthia

Before I could catch my breath, the postman returned from his truck with not one, not two, but three cases of *Honey's Beeswax.* He kindly took them down to the basement, where I stored them next to my stash of promotional copies for *Creola's Moonbeam.*

I looked at the stacked boxes, hands on hips. "You really got me this time, Beatrice! Dear lady, I do thank you with all my being. And I promise, yes, I'll get the book out there for the world to enjoy. The *books.* Plural. *Honey's Beeswax* and *Creola's Moonbeam. Our* books. Yours, mine, and Crellie's."

I knew what I had to do. I walked out into the middle of my front yard. A warm spring night had fallen. I looked up at the moon. To my delight, it was full. Then, without concern for what the neighbors might think, I turned not one, not two, but three cartwheels.

"Thank you, Beatrice," I shouted each time my feet fanned over my head. "Thank you, Crellie."

Falling back onto the grass, I gazed at the moon. There she was, Creola Moon, all light. Silhouetted against her face was a whimsical shadow, a woman doing a cart-wheel. Beatrice. The woman of contradiction and mystery, Beatrice had merged with Creola.

I understood. I would gather my own group of Dear Ones. I would entertain them with my tales, encourage and nurture their talents, and look on as their dreams come true.

I would become their Beatrice, their Creola. I would invite their spirits to join in our circle.

Perhaps, I would even pursue new dreams of my own.

ACKNOWLEDGEMENTS

This thanking folks can be tricky. Especially for me. My paralyzing fear of omitting the names of people supportive and dear kept me from including any acknowledgements whatsoever in my last book, "Ociee on Her Own." That, I truly regret. So here goes.

Many thanks to my fellow authors, Jerry Lee Davis, Jackie White, and Jackie Cooper, with kudos to Jackie Cooper for lining me up with BelleBooks, and with apologies to Jerry Lee for not listening when he made that same suggestion some two years prior!

Thank you, Deb Smith, along with the other amazing women of BelleBooks for believing in Honey Newberry enough to invite me into your circle of authors. Thank you to Martha Crockett for designing "Creola's" lovely cover on the original edition. Thank you to Haywood Smith, again to Jackie and Jackie, and to Charlene Ann Baumbich, Julie Cannon, and Joyce Dixon for your generous remarks about Honey and her fictional family and friends.

Friends. This writer would still have a file full of unused ideas were it not for my real life friends who encouraged me to put words on paper. Thank you, Pam Weeks and Jackie Brown for your prayers, for proofreading "Creola's Moonbeam" and my other three books, and for your years of faith-filled cheerleading.

Thank you also to Betty Ann Colley and Betty George, and to Marc Jolley, Jeff Stives, Carol Lee Lorenzo, and Kristen McGary for always believing in me.

Thank you, Mary and Marvin Brantley, for often introducing me (hope blooms eternal) as "The Margaret Mitchell of Cherrywood Lane" and to Sally Miller for recording, so beautifully, my stories for Books for the Blind.

Thank you to the Marist Moms including Ave, Starr, Ginger, Mary Alyce, Ann, Judi, Linda, Sandy, Patty, Sarah, Jody, Marilyn, and Gail. Also there's the Westfield Garden Club to note, the bridge club, Patty, Kay, Diane, Jean, and JoAnne, our Scripture study class, Clare, AND the ladies of the Artists Way, especially Beverly Key and Janet Wells.

I surely cannot leave out Kristi Hyde, the

Winstons, the Carrolls, the Mittigas, the Lynch or the Davis family, the Jannettas, the Whitmans or the Robnetts, or the Lundys, the Schweitzers . . . or the Birmingham loyal, the Elliotts, the Crums, the Whetstones, the Farrell family, or Diane and Barbara . . . or certainly not the Walthers or the Ekiss family. Oh dear, and there's my beloved Aunt Martha McGraw. Thank you, each and everyone!

With appreciation and love to Kate and Lou, my teachers, my dear ones, and Honey's most ardent advocates.

I conclude by expressing much love to my family, to Jamey, and to Jay, to Amanda, and to Abigail and William, with bunches of kisses for their two little boys, our precious grandsons, Loftin Alan, who's a big brother now four, and for Emmett James, who's grinning his way to age one.

— Milam McGraw Propst

ABOUT THE AUTHOR

Milam McGraw Propst has had careers as a newspaper reporter and feature writer and also in public relations with national companies as well as a variety of volunteer positions.

Highlights for the last several years include the publication of her three books with Mercer University Press: *A Flower Blooms on Charlotte Street, It May Not Leave a Scar,* and *Ociee on Her Own.*

Creola's Moonbeam is her first novel for BelleBooks.

Charlotte Street brought honors to Milam as Georgia Author of the Year for first novel and a nomination for the Townsend Prize for fiction, and nationally, it won the Parents' Choice Fiction Recommendation. As well, the book was made into a motion picture, *The Adventures of Ociee Nash,* starring Mare Winningham, Keith Carradine and Ty Pennington. The film premiered at

Atlanta's Fox Theater on June 1, 2003.

Produced and directed by Amy McGary and Kristen McGary, the film was released nationally in 2004, with the DVD now available. The film introduces Skyler Day as Ociee along with a number of noted Georgia stage actors, including Tom Key, Anthony Rodriquez, Janice Akers, and John Lawhorn.

Milam's short story "Nestle" was published in the March 2004 issue of *Atlanta Magazine*.

Born in Memphis, Tennessee, Milam has also lived in Birmingham, New Orleans, Springfield, Massachusetts, and Atlanta. Married to Jamey Propst, her college sweetheart at the University of Alabama, she has been blessed with three children: Amanda, William, and Jay, and thanks to William and his wife, Abigail, two grandsons, Loftin and Emmett. Notably, the children and Milam were extras in the movie while Jamey netted a small role with some six lines.

Milam currently enjoys public speaking about her books and the film. Contact her via BelleBooks at bellebooks@bellebooks.com.